JUST BEFORE THE DAWN

The darkest hour is . . .

JUST BEFORE THE DAWN

A Hard-boiled Thriller

Bonnie Kozek

LEGACY PUBLISHING LLC

ISBN: 0615443176
ISBN-13: 9780615443171

… when good is hungry it seeks food even in dark caves,
and when it thirsts it drinks even of dead waters.
Khalil Gibran, "Good and Evil"
(from *The Prophet*)

He was wearing a long black coat. The weight of him was angled hard against the side of a burgundy pinstriped Javelin – his boot-heels dug into the dirt, his arms folded across his chest. He was a man waiting on something – and he wasn't in any hurry. However long it took, that's how long it took.

The rim of a black hat dipped low so's I couldn't see his eyes. But he was looking at me all right: when I moved, the hat moved. Uneasy fell on my head like a ton of bricks, and a powerful case of the whim-whams caused my bum leg to gimp up something awful. But I kept on across Interstate 60. And, as I limped nearer him, I felt his eyes bore right through my discomfit and then, well, holey-fucking-moley, if my heart didn't skip a beat and jump right into my throat. And next thing I knew, there we were, standing *mano-a-mano* – nothing between us but a couple of feet and dark bittercold air.

Up close he was kinda squirrelly. Big, greasy – fifty, maybe sixty years old – salt and pepper ponytail and stragglers around the face and chin. His lips were full, pink-brown. His eyes deep-set see-through blue, experienced and wild. There was something familiar in them, but I couldn't say what. They continued to drill into me: *Come a little closer and I'll eat you alive.*

An alien sound escaped my lips – part gasp, part pre-cherry-popping giggle – a sound fit for an unsullied young thing who hadn't had all the innocence drained outta her body long ago – one sorrowful drop at a time. A gal opposite me.

He tilted his head. A shiver ran down my spine.

"Here to prick up a few things." My head swiveled like a bobble-head doll. "I mean, *pick*. *Pick* up a few things."

He didn't respond. He didn't budge. But his crystal unblinking eyes moved slowly over my body – sizing me up, then down – inch by inch. A thick glop of pussy juice soaked right through my panties. I giggled like an idiot and twisted a strand of hair.

"Umm."

And there it was: the sound of his voice.

He stood up – over six feet up – and took a couple of small steps in my direction. He looked down at the ground and kicked the dirt. Then he moved closer.

"I understand," he said slowly, looking me dead in the eyes. "The longest journey . . ." he paused, took a pack of Newports from his pocket, rapped the pack till one stuck out, lit up, took a long drag, exhaled up into the air, then continued. ". . . begins with the first step." He looked down, kicked the dirt, then looked back up at me. "You know what I mean." He spit to the side. "Don't you?"

I should've said something. Really. And I wanted to. But the thing was, I couldn't. I was rattled dumbstruck. There was something about this fella – something particular, extreme, hypnotic. Something in his voice – the grit, the gravel, the determination. Maybe it was the way he took his time – his deliberateness – the pause between his words. Or maybe it was just the grand-prized booty hiding behind that long black coat. *It can be yours if the price is right. Pant. Pant.*

"I said, you know what I mean, don't you?" He wasn't making a polite request this time.

"Well … sure … if … if you say so," I stammered.

He nodded and moved closer – crowding me, horning in. Now, a gal like me – one who doesn't like being corralled or exposed – might've gotten real jumpy and hightailed it outta there right about then, but it was too late: my feet were nailed to the ground.

"Good to see you again," he said.

Again?

He unbuttoned his coat and let it fall open. Underneath was a jogging suit, solid orange, thin fabric – nylon maybe. He unzipped the jacket, baring a chest of wiry hair. Then he bent down and slowly pushed each elastic pant leg up some, exposing tattooed garlands that snaked up his muscled calves. When he reached down inside his pants, my knees went weak. When he purposefully fixed the position of his woody – *just so* – I whimpered.

Sheer willfulness drove me to look up. He was smiling slightly. His eyes were translucent, sparkling – full of unshakable self-command and lust. An apparition suddenly appeared over his head like a bad omen, flashing three words in big bold black letters: **DOUBLE FUCKING TROUBLE**. I caught my breath, exhaling a low slow moan. He leaned back easy against the Javelin and unhurriedly blew perfect round smoke rings into the cold blackness with the vapor of his hot breath. I tried to focus on the disappearing white circles, but I lost my will. My eyes wandered downwards – fixing first on the rhythmic heaving of his chest – up and down, up and down, in and out, in and out – and then finally arriving at the Main Attraction. I stared shamelessly as his cock – aroused solely by the power of his fancy – grew bigger and harder and bigger and harder till it strained so's I thought his pants would split. And just like that, *kowabunga*, I lost my stutter.

"I'm Honey," I said, extending my hand. "Honey McGuinness. Sorry. I don't believe we've met."

He dropped his cigarette and snuffed it with the tip of his boot. Then he gripped my cold hand. The heat of him flooded through my body with the promise of oblivion, an end to all my pain – like a shot in the vein of something sweet, irresistible, illegal – like something I hadn't had in maybe too long a while.

"Ah, you don't remember. It was but yesterday that we met. In a dream."

I was transfixed, lost – hot as a fucking three-dollar pistol.

"I'm sorry. I really don't think I've had the pleasure."

He came so close I could smell his stale gamy breath. Then he closed his eyes and forcefully ran a fat slavering tongue across my mouth.

I made a little sound.

He pushed back some. Then, while staring into my eyes, he guided my hand down the inside of his pants and wrapped it firmly around his hot swollen bozack. He squeezed and moved our hands together – ever so slightly – back and forth along the thick throbbing shaft.

"Well, then, Honey McGuinness." Long pause. "Say hello to Daddy."

Yowza, yowza, yowza.

"Sold this one to Josie Clover, just this afternoon," she announced, pulling a small sand-painting out from behind the counter.

Anita Santa Ana was old and beautiful – full-blooded Pueblo Indian. She owned the only convenience store in town – which carried everything, including the kitchen sink – conveniently named Anita's Convenience Store. She also traded in Indian art.

"She's one lucky dog," I muttered absently, and looked at the sand-painting. My mind was still out on the side of the road.

"This small one's on sale. Five dollars." She set another sand-painting on the counter. It looked something like a buffalo. "That's a fair price."

"Hey, Anita. You see that fella parked on the road, down a-ways?"

She shook her head. "Most likely another one of them Krauts looking for the Grand Canyon." She chuckled, then picked up the sand-painting and extended it towards me. "Five dollars is a fair price."

A German tourist? Hmm. Vater. "Say hello to Vater." *It didn't exactly roll off the tongue, but what the fuck.*

"I could make it four dollars."

I tried to shake off my stupor.

"You don't like it," she said, misinterpreting my wag.

"He was driving a Javelin with orange pinstripes."

"OK. Three dollars. Just for you."

Anita put the sand-painting in my hand, which broke loose some of the muddle.

"Sounds fair and square, bubba."

"Well, how about you buy it then?"

"Not a snowball's chance in hell," I snorted.

She grabbed the painting outta my hand and puffed up some. I started to see her in a different light: larger, stronger, holding a scalp in her hand.

"Hey. Hey. No need to get up on your high-horse. Don't take it personal. I mean, what I know about sand-painting is exactly bupkis."

"You got something against moose, huh?"

"Holy balls. That a moose?" I took it back and examined it closely. "Coulda fooled me."

"You got something against moose, huh?" she repeated, like she was president of the fucking Moose Anti-Defamation League.

I checked the clock on the wall behind her. Two minutes to midnight. The chances of my getting what I came in for and getting out before closing were starting to slim. Maybe some silly would improve my odds.

"I've got nothing against moose. In fact, I speak moose." I grinned.

She snatched the moose outta my hand.

OK. Maybe not. But if Anita thought she was gonna bully me into spending the equivalent of three packs of Ring Dings on that pig-in-a-poke she was passing off as a moose, she had another think coming.

"Tell you what, *amiga*. You get me a box of toothpicks, a carton of Newports, a nail clipper, a fifth of your cheapest rot-gut and some Ring Dings, and I'll am-scray right on outta here." She gave me the ole paleface leather-eye, mumbled something under her breath, and folded her arms across her chest. I could see the writing on the wall.

"You know," I said, knuckling under, "Bullwinkle here is starting to grow on me."

"It's on sale," she smiled, showing dark yellow tar-stained teeth. "Five dollars. Just for you."

"You're tough all over, old woman," I said, and counted my money. I'd have to make a sacrifice. "Skip the Ring Dings."

I lit a smoke and watched the silhouette of a proud Native American woman moving slowly through her store, from one end to the other, shutting off one light at a time. Then I watched while the lights came on in the lodgings above, and after a few minutes, they too went out. The entire building was dark. I inhaled deeply and wondered what it would feel like to be Anita Santa Ana – to be part of history – to have an inherited memory that defined who I was, not as some fucked up atomic swell-head filled with mind-numbing neuroses, but as a whole of something – something that kept its shape whether the lights were on or off. I took a mouthful of forty-rod. It went down like broken glass.

I shuffled along I-60 and parked myself on a bench under the big black-and-white welcome sign: PIE TOWN, Pop. 86. I shook my head and took another slug. *Fuck.* I put my head in my hands. *Double fuck.* I lit another Newport and chewed over my problem.

Just yesterday I was thinking that all in all things were really starting to look up: I got myself a job, a place to hang my hat, even a gal pal. Plus, over the year or so since I'd run outta gas just outside town and decided to stay a spell – particularly since I myself am a pie person – I'd also found what I came looking for – routines, normalcy, anonymity. Now, just cuz a chicken's got wings, doesn't mean it can fly. And I wasn't trying to fool myself. This was no Life of Riley. First off, Lucky Frank's broke-down ole yellow trailer, which I exchanged even-stevens for my broke-down ole yellow Studebaker – the same ole Studebaker that got me balls-to-the-wall outta Skid Row and halfway cross country – had no heat, no hot water, no cooking stove, and lots of leaks. This meant I had to wash up at Alice's Motel – which wasn't so bad, cuz Alice Guthrie took a liking to me and, well, I liked her right back – even though she did have tongue enough for ten rows of teeth: that gal could talk up a shitstorm. Second off, since I couldn't cook my TV dinners, I was living on pie, which meant I was getting myself a nice wide ass – which also wasn't so bad, cuz I needed a little lard in the be-hind if I wanted to fit in with all the other wide-assed gals in town – which was exactly what I wanted to do. So, life wasn't exactly a bowl of cherries, but hey, beggars can't be choosers. Besides, what was wrong with a few trade-offs? As a matter of fact, there was nothing about myself that I didn't want to swap out. But in the trade-off department, I had a problem – one defect that I couldn't give away for free.

I'm fake as a wooden nickel – an imposter, a snake-oil salesman, a phony baloney. I'm uncomfortable in my own skin. I don't have a set picture of who I am. Having a narcissistic homicidal-suicidal lunatic mother and a maggoty bullyboy pedophile father will do that to a gal, I guess. Plus, getting kicked around from foster home to foster home sure doesn't help. See, during those foster years I had a real hankering to belong somewhere, to someone. So I became a chameleon, changing colors to fit in wherever I was. And since I didn't stay in any one place long enough to catch a breath, I became a real quick study. Now, being a quick-study chameleon has its upside: I learned a heap of stuff from some cultured and educated foster-folk.

And, by the time I aged out of the system, well, don't you know, I knew the definition of the word "eclectic," I'd read *Huck Finn* and *The Idiot*, I could speak some Espanola; and I could tell Coltrane from Parker. But all that stuff turns out to be about as useful as a one-legged fella at an ass-kicking party when a gal doesn't know who she is.

Anyways, to correct this little glitch in my personality, I've been trying on different skins – trying to find something that fits. Now this "normalcy" getup, well, I'd been trying real hard to squeeze in, but, like they say, a leopard can't change its spots. So, when my gal pal Alice and I are sitting side by side in the laundromat watching our clothes spin round and round in the side-by-side dryers, Alice actually thinks I'm there with her. But I'm not.

Still and all, at the end of every day, I'm also the gal who's willing to live off of the crumbs, and, like I said, just yesterday I was thinking: *It sure doesn't get any better'n this.* But then I woke up today. And, naturally, today was followed by tonight. And tonight . . . well, I helped some squirrely ole stranger jerk his johnson on the side of I-60 – without a second thought – as if it happened every time I crossed the road – as if it was just some everyday matter of fact – as if it was no great shakes, so to speak.

I took a couple more nips, lit another smoke, and shook my head. No matter how I made the case, it sure did look like I was about to take a header into the shallow end of the pool.

Here it is. This morning I woke up cock-happy. I wanted to ride-the-baloney, pop-a-chop, sink-the-sausage – get banged like a shithouse door in the wind. Now for some other gal, trotting out her Aunt Mary might not seem like much of a predicament. But I'm a sex-equals-death kinda gal, and spreading my legs is deadly as the Black Mamba snakebite. Over the years there'd been plenty of fellas who thought they could beat the odds, but they were wrong . . . dead wrong. So, to save John Q. Public the misery, I figured I'd stay offa men – which was exactly what I'd done for a month of Sundays – save for that time a while back when some lowlife crack-dealing mucker ploughed my back forty, which doesn't really count cuz, well, some fuckathons just don't count. Anyways, the truth is: I was happy to give up the flesh. It was a relief. But as of this morning, all that changed. Now sex was oozing out my pores. My body was aching with hunger. Forget playing solitaire. I wanted the real thing: I wanted a man. And it was a damned bloody shame.

When I got back to my trailer I gave myself a nice warm soapy enema – the one thing I could always count on to set my head straight. But this time it was too little too late. *Fuck.* I threw on my old ratty black coat and went out for a walk.

■ ■ ■

I knew right away it was him. He was in just the right place at just the right time, and just blotto enough not to make a stink. I mounted him right there on the hard cold gravel alongside I-60. I rode him like Senor Speedy in the Derby – high, low, and sideways. I stood him up, rolled him over, and nailed him to the ground. Me and old baldy got as close as two coats of paint. And when I took him across the finish line I knew I'd given him one helluva ride – one he wouldn't soon be forgetting. He never made a sound, but the whites of his teeth sparkled beneath a grin that stretched from ear to ear across his perfectly pocked face, and lit up the blackness of the high desert night like a supernova. I stood up and drained the last of my hooch.

He sat up, reached for his Stetson, and started humming "Amazing Grace."

I laughed.

"Chalk it up to dumb luck, mister."

He shook his head.

"What, then?"

He smiled big.

"God's good grace, missy."

I gimped off across the butte back to my trailer with my head down and my tail between my legs. It wasn't that dumb luck Lucky Frank was a total washout. It was that he was an also-ran: I had Daddy on the brain. *Oh, Daddy. Who are you?*

"Lordy, Lordy, girl! You are a pisser!"

Alice was hovering over me, her mollycoddled mongrel Romeo in her arms – like usual. Being that she weighed three-twenty on a pie-less day and the mutt was about as big as a peanut, they made quite a pair. Since her identical twin boys hotfooted it outta Pie Town the day after their sixteenth birthday – never to be seen again – and her no-good alky husband forsook her long before, Romeo was a stand-in for Mr. Wrong and the wayward brats. The way she let the cur "kiss" her mouth after licking his pea-sized nuts was enough to make a gal puke. But like I said, I liked Alice, and besides, a gal who'd just recently jacked off some squirrelly stranger on the side of the road wasn't rightly qualified to judge whose tongue should go where.

The sun was blinding, my head was throbbing, and I was wound up tight as a tick.

"Can it, Alice. I'm in no mood."

It's true. Even though I'd sharpened Lucky Frank's pencil but good last night, I didn't get off – which isn't exactly breaking news to me, but it might've been to Lucky Frank, cuz I faked it pretty good – just like I used to before I gave up the flesh. Funny how easy it was to fool a fella; ten seconds of panting, some head rolling, a little wheezing, and then, of course, the Big Finish. I didn't like it much that I could only get off by my lonesome, but that's just the way the cookie crumbled. But last night – after balling Lucky Frank – no matter how hard I worked – and I sure did give it my best – inserting anything and everything I could get my hands on into my chucky – I couldn't climax. So, I cried Uncle and did something I knew I could do – drink myself unconscious. And apparently I did it so good that I was still spread-eagle on the tiny kitchen table with my arms and legs dangling over the edges and my g-string down around my ankles when Alice came a-calling.

"Don't look," Alice said to Romeo, covering his eyes. "You're too young for this, my little man."

The little runt nuzzled her hand away and ogled me like I was his bitch. Alice slapped her thigh and hooted.

"Last I remember, no one asked you skulkers in." I lifted my chin. "Don't let the door hit you where the good Lord split you."

She slapped her thigh and hooted again.

I struggled to get up, and my hairbrush – the most unsatisfying lover at last night's disappointing orgy – which hadn't until then found its way out of my pussy – fell to the floor, and my leg buckled and Alice caught me before I collapsed, using one-armed muscle to lift me to my feet. And then, cuz I wasn't humiliated enough, I took a couple of steps forward and wouldn't you know it, I was as bowlegged as a buckaroo. Alice nearly died laughing. I gave her the dead-eye and grabbed a towel to cover myself.

When Alice caught her breath she said, "What in the name of the Good Lord Jesus Christ happened to you? What in the –"

I gave her the "time-out" sign, warning that she'd better knock it off and pipe down if she knew what was good for her. She rolled her eyes and said "Oh, Lordy" under her breath a couple more times and set Romeo down. He immediately sniffed out my hairbrush, then gave it lick. Alice hooted. I reached for the bottle of rot-gut. Painfully, it was empty. I lit a Newport and inhaled deeply.

"*What the hell!?*" Alice asked accusingly, grabbing Romeo up and pulling him tight against her lumpy flesh like she'd just seen the boogie man.

"What the hell what?" I asked, though I knew good and well what the hell what was.

"You're . . . *drinking!* You're . . . *smoking!* Since when –"

"Since it was none of your beeswax, which is always."

She started to bawl. *Shit.* I should've figured Miss Sensitive was gonna take it hard, being that her ex was a boozehound who took her for every penny she had and left her alone to run the motel and raise a couple of unmanageable toddlers; and being that she was the child of alcoholics and chain smokers; and being that she found her father drowned in a bathtub after a week of binging; and being that she watched her mother die a slow, agonizing death from lung cancer – well, I guess she had a right to be a little touchy on these particular subjects. And I didn't want to hurt her, but hey . . . it was my life, my death . . . not hers. Besides, what was I gonna say?

The truth was that I hadn't had a drink or a smoke since I hit Pie Town over a year ago. But it's also true that I'm a stone cold junkie. Consequently, when it comes to vices – felonious, narcotic, carnal, or otherwise sinful – well, it's All or Nothing. And as of yesterday, it became All – which was exactly how it was gonna stay till I drank myself into a coma, smoked till I needed a ventilator, and fucked myself brainless. Now the good news – if under the circumstances there was such a thing – is that I'm no addict, and I've got a real selective memory. As a result, once I've had my fill of any particular nastiness, I tend to forget, lose interest. And once I lose interest, that's it: it's over. Cold turkey. But somehow I didn't think any part of my explanation would give Alice much comfort, so I kept it to myself.

As we shuffled across the butte to the motel, she sulked. It wouldn't last. Alice was a sweetheart: she couldn't hold a grudge. Plus, she sure did love to hear the sound of her own voice. I didn't mind the quiet. Fact the silence was a mercy, cuz at the moment I had bigger fish to fry: *Daddy. Oh, where are you, Daddy? When will I see you again? Will I see you again?* Since Alice had her nose in everyone's business, she'd be the one to ask about the man in the long black coat – which was exactly what I intended to do just as soon as she quit her moping. I laughed to myself. If the man in the long black coat turned out to be just another Kraut who got lost in Pie Town cuz he couldn't read a roadmap, well, warning local cowmen: *Honey Hot Pants is gunnin' for you!*

We stopped in the motel office. Under normal circumstances, Alice was quick to give me a room key so's I could wash up. Not today. She moved about as fast as a dead snail.

"Hmm," she said, flipping through the motel registry one page at a time – as if there weren't nine vacancies in the nine-room motel, just like every other day.

"Aw, c'mon, Alice." I tilted my head and blinked. "Don't be sore."

She mumbled something about what a fool she was to think there might've actually been one person in the world that she loved who didn't turn out to be a bloody sot. I might've said I loved her too, but I couldn't. See, when it came to "loving" persons of the same sex, well, things were even more balled up than with the opposite sex. Unlike the hapless fellas who'd fallen for me, no gal had ever ended up in a body-bag, with the exception, of course, being my mother. But still, even if you couldn't see their wounds, they were there – deep and wide. Still, I was touched that Alice cared, and if there ever was a gal in the world I would've wanted to love without hurting, well, it would've been big ole good-natured Alice Guthrie.

She slammed the registry shut, reached back, and dropped a key just outta reach. I waited.

"You're a pain in my back-end," she said, shaking her head.

I shrugged.

"I swear, if today wasn't your big day, I'd hose you down, hang you on the line, and let you drip-dry!"

She tried not to smile but failed. She turned and disappeared into the back room.

While she was gone I mindlessly fingered the mail on the counter. Bills. Advertisements. Personal letter. *Personal letter?* That got my attention. I picked it up. The envelope was handwritten; the sender's name was missing. There was no return address. I held it up to the light. It was written on lined paper. The only words I could make out clearly were "Dear Mama." I checked the postmark. I couldn't make out the name of the town. There was a broken, wavy line above an illegible name and below that a solid line. *Hmm.* I'd seen this postmark somewhere before. But where? When? I strained my brain. It was no use. Bupkis.

I heard the familiar sound of Alice shuffling. She had Romeo tucked under one arm, and a clean towel, a bar of soap, and a washcloth under the other. *What a pal.* I quickly slid the letter under the pile of mail: if Alice had something to tell me, she'd tell me.

"OK, *amigos* and *amigas*. Let's settle down and get this show on the road!"

The small crowd hushed. I looked around. Everyone came out for me – even Lucky Frank, whose provocative grin turned my face redder than a baboon's ass.

Master of ceremonies United States Marshal Duncan Hayward – known around town as Dunk – gave me a good-ole-boy slap on the back. He forgot about my bum leg, and I went down. He apologetically helped me back up onto my feet. I dusted myself off. This was my moment in the sun, and nothing was gonna cloud it over.

"Maybe if we do this fast we'll get 'er done this time!" Dunk chuckled, his big belly shaking like jelly.

"Third time's a charm," shouted Alice, no longer brooding.

"We all know why we're here today," Dunk said. "So without further ado—"

Someone shouted. The crowd murmured and turned. It was Forrest "Fob" Johnson, U.S. census-taker and head of the state Land & Records Office. He was running towards us and waving something in his hand.

"Hold up, Dunk," he hollered.

A ripple of "Oh, no" and "Not again" spread through the crowd.

Oh yes. Again.

This was the third time that Fob Johnson had disrupted the ceremony that would've painted out the number 86 on the Pie Town welcome sign, and painted on the number 87 – which would've made me an "official" and "duly recorded" citizen of Pie Town – which would've proven that I, Honey McGuinness, finally counted. But just like the other two times, Fob announced that the town was short one "resident" – this time, Daisy Clover, who'd left town a couple of weeks ago, the day after her eighteenth birthday – which meant that once again and still, the population of Pie Town was 86. The sign would not be changed.

■ ■ ■

I hobbled, bowlegged, over to a nearby bench and watched the crowd mosey off down the road. Alice stopped by and patted my head and told me one day I'd be number 87 and till then I should keep my pecker up. Fuck her. Fuck this town. *What was wrong with these folks? Why couldn't they keep their fucking offspring around long enough to get me rubber-stamped?*

OK. Maybe Pie Town had its downsides. I mean, size-wise it was barely big enough to swing a cat. And it had definitely seen better days. It straddled a neglected and unused interstate, but back in the 1940s the town was full to bursting – about 250 families – and the thoroughfare was flush with coupes and sedans and Pontiac Woodys. The folk were of an independent ilk – mostly come from Texas to flee the Dust Bowl and the Depression. It was a rough-and-tumble place then – all-night boozing and dancing, no running water, no electric, homes made of mud and logs. But things changed. During World War II, when there was plenty of work in munitions plants and a long drought, most families moved on. Nowadays near everyone was on the government dole and most businesses were long gone. The last one to close up shop was H&R Block, cuz, as Alice put it, "Even if you don't have a pot to piss in, they still expect you to pay taxes!" OK, so maybe Pie Town didn't have the big draws of other small towns across the U.S. of A. – like a two-story outhouse or the world's largest thermometer or a drive-through strip club – but it had its own magic. Big skies and lightning fields. And great fucking pie.

There're two accounts of how Pie Town got its name. One contends that a family with a wagonload of dried fruit and flour got lost on their way to Californ-I-A and decided to plant roots. Being a waste-not-want-not pioneering kinda gal, the wife of this clan decided to make the very first pies in Pie Town out of the dried fruit before it went to rot. The other story has a drunken cowman declaring "This must be Pie Town!" Either way, the name stuck – but not without objection. The folks didn't take kindly to the name cuz they didn't think it accurately rendered the machismo of the place. So's the Pie Town postman wrote a letter, personally, to the U.S. Postmaster

General in Washington D.C., begging him to change the name, saying it was "ridiculous" and "below the dignity" of the United States Postal Service. But, like I said, it stuck.

Anyhow, neither Pie Town's kin nor its meager attractions were enough to keep their pubescent ingrates from hauling ass outta town, helter-skelter – leaving behind a populace of young fries and old fries and nothing in between – 'cept for me, the only gal in town in her twenties. And as for me, well, I didn't have a hurry-on to run after fame and fortune. I was partial to life in the slow lane. I liked the ordinariness. I liked how the common folk weren't dumb enough to think they were better or smarter or more good-looking than the next guy – cuz they were sharp enough to know that there was always gonna be someone better or smarter or more beauteous than they were. I liked how there was no humbuggery – no delusional over-bloated gasbags running around bragging about how they were gonna change the world. I don't know. I guess you could say they were content with their lot. And I guess you could say I envied them that.

Still and all, here I was . . . down and out. *What the fuck*? Why did I even care? I mean, what was the big fucking deal about becoming an "official" citizen of Pie Town – or an "official" *anything* for that matter? *Fuck*. I shook my head. It was all Skinner's fault – Officer Skinner P. Ochs.

■ ■ ■

I met Skinner over a year ago when I was living on Skid Row. The two of us got into a tight jam, and fuck if the flatfoot didn't put his life on the line for me – take a bullet to the head for me – save my life. And what did I do? Shit a cold purple Twinkie, that's what. Cowered, groveled, begged a couple of lowlife scum-sucking thugs for my miserable little life. Oh yes I did. And after that act of spinelessness, I felt exposed. Skinner knew the truth about me: when push came to shove, I was just another flimflam Charley Hunt. Now being that Officer Ochs was what you'd call a true gentleman, he never rubbed my nose in my cowardice. But still, just looking at him started to make me sick. Physical sick. The kinda sick a gal gets when a fella knows too much about her – when all she can see when she looks into this fella's eyes is her own sorry reflection. And then worse happened: he got under my skin. And, well, after a while, I just couldn't stand it. I couldn't stand feeling soft and sweet when I was around him. I couldn't stand that he was big and goofy as a wild baby bear. That he was happily married. That he had Faith. That I couldn't ever have him. I couldn't even stand that he wanted to give me something I'd never had before – love that didn't hurt. So, I slunk off into the sunset, leaving Mr. Perfect – with his Perfectly Fetching Wife, his Perfectly Adorable Girls, and his Perfectly Ordinary Life – without so much as an *adios pardner*. But it's funny. Not in the funny-ha-ha kinda way, though. I mean, something about Officer Skinner P. Ochs stuck in me. See, Mr. Holier-Than-Thou made me think that maybe, just maybe, we *were* all part of some divine plan. And for the first time in my pathetic little life I thought, well, maybe the fucker's right. Maybe, just maybe, I can be part of the plan. Maybe I can be normal – go to work and watch TV. Maybe I can eat and fuck and sleep. Maybe I can have faith and go to church. Maybe I can have a real life. Maybe I can have it all – just like everyone else. Yeah, before Mr. Goody-Fucking-Two-Shoes got inside my head I didn't give a flying fuck about anything. Now look at me: crying over a digit.

I lit a smoke and stood up. It was almost noon. Time to get shit-faced.

"I won't abide intemperance, young lady!"

Puritanical, God-fearing, flaming red-headed Maggie Horton, along with her quadriplegic husband Tommy – a fella I'd never actually seen cuz he never came down from their upstairs apartment – was white enough to give me a job tending bar at the El Serape, and at the moment she was none too pleased with me. She grabbed for the bottle, and we played tug o'war till she gave.

"I won't stand for this drunkenness in my establishment!" Maggie added, smoothing her hair back from her comely face.

I took a swig and laughed. "Establishment? Hardy har. You mean gin mill chophouse, dontcha?"

"I told you when I hired you," she stomped her foot. "No drinking on the job!"

"Yeah? Well, how about your *Save-Yer Geeeee-zuss Chr-rist*?" I took another swig. "I think he did a little drinking on the job." I took another swig and laughed. "I seen the picture of that last supper!"

"Blasphemer! Watch your mouth, young lady!"

"Lady, schmady."

"Well, I never!"

"That is a real shame, Miss Priss," I tittered, not at all surprised that she "never."

I waved the bottle in her face, came out from behind the bar, and tottered across the room. "Whaddya say Punchclock?" I slurred.

Pasty-white, skinny-as-a-rail Buddy Pinchback – who I called "Punchclock" just to get his goat – postmaster of the tumbledown Pie Town Post Office, was the only fella in the establishment, sitting at his table, alone, and eating the daily lunch special, like he did every day. He was just about to eat a spoonful of banana cream pie.

"Go home. Sleep it off," he said coldly.

"C'mon, Punchclock. I'll go if you come with me. Whaddya say? Help me *sleep it off*, if you know what I mean?"

"Lord have mercy!" Maggie said.

I sat in Buddy's lap, which caused the pie to fall off the spoon. He pushed me and I landed in the chair next to him.

"The strong silent type," I said to Maggie. I chuckled, and a little drool trickled down my chin. I wiped it off and pinched Buddy's cheek. "C'mon, don't be shy, Punchclock."

Buddy glared at Maggie – to let her know I was a no-good lowlife lard-ass pain in his neck. Then he patted his mouth with the edge of his napkin like he was some aristo-fucking-crat, put some small change on the table, picked up his mailbag, and started to leave.

"*Please, please, Mister Postman . . . look and see, oh yeah . . . if there's a letter, oh yeah . . . in the bag for me,*" I sang off-key, and then snatched the bag outta his hand.

Maggie came across the room and grabbed my arm.

"The Devil's gotten into her!"

"I wish someone *would* get into me!"

I nearly bust a gut at my own stupid joke while the three of us tussled back and forth, and Maggie kept yelling about the Devil getting into me and asking me when it was that I took up drinking and I told her to put a sock in it, and then the mailbag ripped and the contents fell to the floor, which pushed me right over the edge into hysteria.

"Poor little letters," I laughed and blubbered at the same time, trying to catch my breath.

Then I bent over to pick up the letters, but my bum leg gave and I fell flat on my keester – right on top of the poor little letters. Buddy and Maggie harrumphed. Then they each took an arm and pulled me to my feet.

"Tampering with U.S. mail is a Category Three misdemeanor. Section thirteen point four one one," Buddy warned, scooping up the mail.

Hmm. Section thirteen point four one one. I knew that. How did I know that?

"Don't get your ass in an uproar," I hiccuped, looking at the letter that had somehow ended up in my hand. It was addressed to "Pop & Josie Clover" – parents of Pie Town's most recent fugitive, Daisy Clover. Handwritten. No return address. Postmark a broken black wavy line above illegible letters. Suddenly I felt sober.

"That's weird," I said, looking at the postman.

"You're like a bad penny – always turning up," he muttered. Then he grabbed the letter and marched out in a huff.

"Buenos nachos, *Punchclock*," I whispered in his ear as he passed.

"See you tomorrow, Buddy?" Maggie called after him hopefully.

I contended with Maggie a while longer, but it was no use. No way she was gonna let me stay out my shift, cuz I was "filled with wickedness." Plus she wasn't gonna let me drink up her profits – even after I pointed out that as the inventor of El Serape's best-selling cocktail, The Pie Slicer – which at four and a half bucks a pop made it the most expensive and profitable drink in the house – I had earned a few fucking free shots.

■ ■ ■

I stopped at Anita's to pick up some cheap hooch. Then, as I ambled back to the trailer, I thought about Buddy's warning about tampering with the mail. *Sure sounded familiar.* Then it hit me . . . a conversation I'd had with him, maybe a month or so before . . .

. . . I'd stopped by to pick up my mail – which was a big fucking joke, cuz I never had any. Still, *everybody* went to the post office, and since it was my single purpose to be just like *everybody*, I went too. When Buddy went into the back to get my mail – which ordinarily consisted of two or three advertisements and special coupons for supermarkets in Springerville, and something addressed to "or current resident" – I looked at the mail on the counter. As usual, there was a stack of newsletters entitled *The Fourth Wave*, published by one of the churches in town that claimed to have "The Answer" to "The Question." Alice always took a copy of *The Fourth Wave*. She'd give it a quick read on the way out of the post office and say an "Amen" or two – which I would dutifully echo. I'd never actually read the rag, cuz when it came to God, well, I guess you could say I was another anti-God dumbass – until, that is, a certain Mister Perfect-Faith Skinner P. Ochs came into my life. And I guess you could say that after we met I became a little less of an anti-God dumbass, but not much less. Plus, I didn't even know what "The Question" was, let alone "The Answer." Plus, every time I looked at the newsletter I got kinda depressed cuz it reminded me that I was a no one: there was a box in the upper right corner on the front page that read: Pie Town, Pop. 86. So anyways . . . That day at the post office I sifted through the few pieces of mail left on the counter, and that's when I noticed it: every piece had the Springerville postmark – except one. It was a handwritten letter, addressed to Caudill Jackson.

"Where's this from?" I asked when Buddy returned, pointing out the postmark.

That's when he told me about section thirteen point four one one. And that's when he told me I was a "God-damned busybody" and I should keep my nose out of other people's business and if I didn't he'd tell U.S. Marshal Duncan Hayward that I was tampering with the United States mail. I laughed right in his face.

Anyhoo, at the moment I couldn't be bothered thinking about Buddy Pinchback or the funny-looking postmark. I was hot in the tail – and I wasn't looking forward to another lonely night of ungratifying finger-fucking and enemas. I didn't think my Aunt Mary or my winking-walnut could take another go-round. However, they could have a change of heart ... if *he* were to show up. *Oh, Daddy. Who are you?* Maybe I'd never know. As it turned out, my best hope – my only hope – Miss Alice-Nosey-Parker – didn't know jack about the man in the long black coat or his pinstriped Javelin.

The sky was day-glow orange and ultramarine blue. In the distance over the pass I could see lightning bolts streaking through a black-gray patch of sky. It happened like that – right in the middle of the day – just in that spot – the lightning spot. Across the field a dog and cat were playing in the dirt. Just a day ago I would've said, *This is the life*. But not now. I was totally fixated. All I could think about was flesh. Flesh on flesh. Sex. Fucking. Something real and hard moving in and out of my hot, wet pussy. And I wanted it from Daddy. And it was a crying shame, cuz if I really thought about it, well, how could I compare the short-term mercy of a few minutes of carnal pleasure to a lifetime of normalcy? But that was just the thing: I couldn't think anymore.

To tell the truth, I was sick about the whole thing – about losing my desire to get normal. Sure, it'd been tricky, but it was also non-toxic. And now ... now I was pathological, phobic – already drinking and smoking and obsessing to excess. And I knew this was just the beginning. I'd been down this rabbit hole before, and I knew it was gonna be a long dangerous drop till I finally hit bottom. I heaved a big sigh. I guess when it comes to gals like me it's never too late to go wrong.

In my dream I'm a fish – a whole fleshy fish – and I'm looking to get filleted. I need to find a slicing machine like the ones used for loaves of meat and cheese. A young boy helps me locate a machine and shows me how to use it, then leaves me alone. I push my fleshy fish self against the cold metal plate and the sharp blade slices off my head and then trims my belly and then lops off my top scales. And when I'm done I'm a perfectly trimmed fish fillet.

■ ■ ■

I woke up in a cold sweat. It was dark outside. Two bare hanging lightbulbs lit up the dingy trailer: I never could sleep in the dark. I was hungover and my head was splitting. I sat up and looked in the mirror. I was wearing a black g-string, garter belt, stockings, low-cut bra, and black velvet high heels strapped at the ankles. My hair was loose and messy. Red lipstick was smeared across my mouth. It'd been one helluva a night – lonely and over-sexed, and, just like I figured it would be, a total flop.

I stood up and looked in the mirror. The face looking back at me was sad. She looked like she'd been crying her whole life. She was a pitiable creature with two sorrowful eyes – the eyes of a small child – stuck in the body of a grown woman – a woman all fleshy and ripe and delicious. They were the eyes of a child frozen in the exact moment when the pain became so unbearable, so unspeakable, that even her silent tears could no longer call out for help. And although she was a big girl now, her soul was unable to escape what her body had outgrown – and her little eyes continued to tell the story of a lifetime of horror heaped upon the little girl, layer upon layer, spilling over . . . until there was nothing left but the defenseless victim, the willingly tormented, the helplessly starved, the unavoidably withered.

I looked around. A small clip-on fan, a portable stereo component system with auto-reverse, a few pieces of tattered clothing, two sealed cardboard boxes – these were all my worldly possessions. I stared at the boxes. I hated myself for carting them all the way to Pie Town, but I got used to hating myself long ago and, hell, well, everyone's gotta be good at something.

It was a Raven 25 – black with an imitation mother-of-pearl handle. It cost me a double sawbuck. It held six rounds, plus one in the chamber. The small-time wannabe hood I copped it from had no problem selling the "Saturday Night Special" to a messed-up teen, or showing her how to lock, load, and shoot to kill. I'd only fired it twice. I checked the magazine: four bullets. I checked the chamber: one. I wrapped it back up in dark, musty fabric that was cracked at the folds and set it aside while I continued to search the box. I pulled out a few news clippings about a dead man found in the backseat of his red Pontiac Firebird – a single bullet hole in the head. They retrieved a .25 caliber slug from his brain, but there were no leads and the killer was never caught. They said the man was victim of a robbery; his wallet was missing. Then I pulled out a thin black billfold, two sawbucks and a fin still in the inside pocket. I removed the driver's license: Mike McGuinness. Height: Six-foot-six. Weight: One-ninety-seven. Eyes: Blue. Hair: Brown. It belonged to the dead man.

I shot my father in the head when I was just a snot-nosed pubescent cuz – being that I was a dead ringer for my mother, the love of his life and the woman who gave him the old heave-ho – well, he thought it was perfectly all right to use me as a stand-in for his sexual needs. And by the time I was six years old, long after my mother'd thrown the bum out, he sure was needing a lot of sex. I never lived with him, though. Not even after my crackbrained homicidal-suicidal mother took a swan dive off a fourth-floor balcony – at which time I punked out and shook free of her grip, despite the fact that I'd taken a sacred oath to die with her – which, at the time I took it, seemed better than the alternative, which was to die *by* her. No, my father didn't want me fulltime, even then. So, after that – after I punked out and after my mother landed with a thud and I tumbled down some concrete stairs so's she could die in my arms and so's I could keep my mouth shut and play the hero when the cops assumed that I'd taken the leap with her and miraculously survived – me and my bum leg and my limp were shipped off to one foster home after another. But my father kept an eye on me. He came to get me every weekend – and sometimes in between. And, after a decade or so of being his personal sex toy, I decided to even the score. That's when I copped the Raven.

It was winter. My father pitched pebbles at my bedroom window. I was ready. Like usual, I snuck outta bed and tiptoed into the dark of night to meet him at the corner. He drove to our "secret spot" – a secluded corner of a park a couple miles away. When he told me to be a "good girl" and hop on into the backseat with him . . . well, that's when I tilted my head and said, "Some good girls go bad." He looked confused. But he got enlightened real quick: I popped a cap right between his eyes. I ran back to the house, stopping only to bury my PJs, the gun, and his wallet in a hole I'd dug in the backyard near an old oak tree. Then I slipped back into the house, into clean PJs, and back into bed unnoticed.

His body was discovered the next morning, and when my foster parents gave me the tragic news, I cried just like a baby. Since we were all home asleep at the time of the shooting, the cops didn't ask me a single question. *Ha.* A couple of months later I was shipped off to another foster home. I took my belongings with me – packed in cardboard boxes. But now I had one more, smaller than the others. It held a cheap loaded pistol wrapped in bloodstained PJs, a man's wallet, and a couple of newspaper clippings.

I never expected to use the Raven again. But, well, shit happens. I looked across at the unopened box in the corner: it told the story of that shit. I lit a Newport and shrugged. I don't know, maybe some secrets never get told. But what I do know is that when it comes to pedophiles and evil motherfuckers, two dead bodies are better than one.

Anyways, I was feeling as jumpy as a cat on a hot tin roof. I put the stuff back and resealed the box. Then I set it right back where I'd found it. I could've easily chucked it. I mean, I'd already trashed other boxes – bigger boxes – boxes containing secrets just as dark. But I couldn't let go of this one. Someway the physical evidence in this little box had warped into a monstrous perversion – proof that I once had a father, proof that he once loved me. I wiped tears and snot from my face and took a few chugs of rot-gut. I put on John Lee Hooker and listened to "On the Waterfront." But it didn't matter. The sickening truth was the sickening truth: I still wanted to be daddy's "good girl."

■ ■ ■

I staggered out to the phone booth on I-60. It was the middle of the night and I was skunk drunk, but still I made the call . . . collect.

"Yes. Yes, of course I will," she said to the operator. Her voice was tender, sleepy, concerned. "Honey? Honey, is that *really* you?"

I mumbled incomprehensibly.

"Oh, God! Honey, are you all right?" She suddenly sounded wide awake.

"Don't worry, no one died," I hiccupped. "Sorry I woke you."

"No, no, no! No apologies," she said sincerely. "I can't even *tell* you how good it is to hear your voice! I've missed you *soooo* much!"

I felt sick in the stomach. Mary was so genuine – so kindhearted. Not a fake bone in her body. Me? A sleazy heartless shammer: it wasn't Mary I wanted to talk to – it wasn't Mary I was missing – it was her faithful husband Skinner P. Ochs. I grunted.

"Well, where are you, for goodness' sake? Are you all right? We've been *so* worried—"

"A-OK. Fine and dandy," I slurred.

"Oh, Skinner is going to be so upset he missed your call."

My heart sank. "But … it's the middle of the night," I complained, miserably.

"Oh, you know how it is. The life of a policeman. He's been working graveyard for the longest time."

I felt like I'd been kicked in the gut.

"We miss you, Honey. Skinner *always* talks about you, and the girls are *always* asking when you're coming over for dinner."

Skinner always talks about me? What does he say? Does he tell you he loves me? Does he tell you he wants me in the worst way?

"Honey? Are you there?"

"Bless their little hearts," I managed.

She laughed heartily. "So, tell me. Where *are* you? And when are you coming home?"

"Home?" I repeated, as if I'd never heard the word before.

"Sorry. I didn't hear you. Where are you?" she asked again.

I took a deep inhale and a long exhale, trying to resign myself to the fact of the matter: it had taken me over a year to get up the grit to make this call, and now Skinner wasn't even there.

"I didn't get that. Sorry. Where are you?" she asked a third time.

"The land of enchantment," I said, without any enchantment.

"You're kidding! I swear, we were *just* talking about a trip . . ."

I lost her to static.

"What?"

"What?"

"Did you say something about a trip?"

"Yes. But God only knows when Skinner will get some time off – if ever! He'd sure love to take the girls camping – show them the Aztec ruins and Carlsbad and the Painted Cave. His pa took him on just such a trip when he was about Rosa's age. But, of course, it all depends . . ."

Mary continued talking, but recollections of Skinner started to flood my mind. The way he looked at me with his big blue eyes, made bigger by thick bifocals. The way he'd summon up some profound words of wisdom that he learned from his pa – always at just the right moment. The way he loved his ma and pa. The way he was once a boy and grew up into a man. The way he never gave up on God or stayed angry . . . even after his folks burned to death in a house fire while he was off to school.

"What town did you say you're in?"

"Pie Town," I answered, mindlessly.

She laughed full and throaty. "Oh, you're so funny!"

Funny like a train wreck.

"No, seriously, where are you?"

"West Bum Fuck."

Static interrupted the connection.

"What? What town?" she asked again.

"Anyhoo . . ." I said, ready to end the conversation.

Static jammed the line again. When it cleared she was saying again that Skinner was gonna be real upset that he missed my call and that if she didn't find out how he could get back in touch with me there was gonna be hell to pay. It wasn't true. Skinner would never give Mary hell to pay. I knew that cuz one night back on the Row, Skinner came crying to me when Mary pulled the rug out from under him – made him doubt God and every godly thing he ever believed in – by having an abortion behind his back. And even then – with nothing more than just a couple of phony-baloney platitudes of the feminist ilk from yours truly – he'd forgiven her everything. No, I knew Mary was just laying it on thick to make me feel good. Cuz when it came to Mary, "too good to be true" wasn't.

"Ah, forget it, Mary. Don't even bother. Look, I gotta run. I got someone waiting on me."

"You've met someone! That's wonderful! Tell me all about him! I want details!"

"Welp, I met him at church and he's as handsome as Prince Charming, and . . ." It suddenly struck me that I'd told her the name of the town I was in and I hit myself in the forehead with the receiver. I don't know why. I guess part of my fancy was that Skinner would come looking for me if he only knew where I was. It wasn't true, of course, but I tweaked my story anyways, ". . . and we're hitting the road *manana*. Taking off for parts unknown."

"Oh, Honey, will you *ever* settle down?"

"Home is where you live, not where you love," I slurred.

"What? What was that?"

I listened to her breathing through the static for a moment. I didn't wanna repeat what I'd said cuz I wasn't sure I got it right, plus saying it made my heart ache something awful. It was one of those hokey sayings that Skinner had repeated to me back on Skid Row when things got rough. Funny how hokey from the mouth of the right fella can make everything all better.

I hung up on Mary and leaned my head against the phone box. I made that stupid silent crying face – the one with my mouth hung open and tears coming down but no sounds. After a while I wiped the snot dangling from my nose and headed back across the butte.

Light from the single small window of my trailer tunneled down onto the ground, creating an elongated rectangle in the darkness. At the edge of the rectangle I noticed a shape. As I lumbered forward the shape came into focus . . . a man . . . wearing a long black coat . . . leaning against a pin-striped Javelin. *Yippee yi-o ki-a.*

"I would've come sooner . . . but I knew you'd take some time."

I blinked and tilted my head. He wiped the tears from my face. There was no pity in him.

"Some *time*?" I asked.

"Umm."

He licked his lips. My face flushed red and a weird sound escaped my mouth. He stepped closer and looked into my eyes.

"You're not easy, Honey McGuinness. You're a voyage. A long, long voyage."

He reached out and pressed his hand against my heart. I got hotter than a red-assed bee.

"Oh, no . . . no," I stuttered. "I mean . . . uh . . . I'm not a long voyage. I'm not even a short trip. I'm just plain old ordinary—"

"You're wrong about that. '*Her price is far above rubies.*' There's nothing ordinary or plain about you. You are a rosebud – a diamond. Intricate. Complicated. Labyrinthine."

I giggled like a half-witted labyrinthine, whatever that was.

"Like they say, we've howdied, but we ain't shook yet." He extended his hand. "Creed Kurgan," he grinned wickedly, "but you can call me . . ."

He waited for me to fill in the blank.

"Daddy." *Pant. Pant.*

He smiled broadly and nodded. I took hold of his hand and my knees went weak. Touching his flesh took my breath away. He was sizzling. I thought about how good it would feel to have his hot blood pumping through my veins, keeping me warm. I was always so cold inside. He held my hand firmly, like he had the other night when it was wrapped around his big hard who-who-dilly. He had the might of a great solid oak – potent, heroic, wise. I pictured him fucking me. *How sweet it is.*

"How did you—"

"It's a small town," he answered. "You weren't hard to find."

"You were . . . *are.* No one seems to know you. I asked around."

He grimaced disapprovingly.

"Well, actually, I only asked one person," I explained apologetically.

"I live in a hole and corner."

"Fancy that," I said and smiled sweetly.

He took a step back and looked me up and down. He was appraising my body. I fidgeted. He moved closer and lifted my chin.

"I see your halo."

I laughed out loud. "Not a Chinaman's chance!"

"No?" he said. "Then you must be a sinner."

"Now you're talkin'!"

"*'Your sins are more than you can bear.'*"

I giggled like a half-wit again.

"Only the sinner has a right to preach. If I ask for a certain thing, it will be done. Right?"

What the Sam Hill?

"If I ask for a certain thing, it will be done. Right?" he repeated.

Aha. A little s-e-x-game. OK, as long as he feeds the kitty, I'm all in.

I nodded enthusiastically.

"I didn't hear you."

"Your wish is my command!" I saluted.

His scowled. I dropped my salute. He waited.

"I mean, yes," I said, correcting my displeasing perkiness.

"Good girl."

And there it was. Pathological fantasy fulfilled. He called me his "good girl." I was daddy's good girl!

"Now, come to Daddy."

He made a sound I'd never heard before – not human, not animal. He ran his fingers across my lips, up and down the sides of my face, through my hair, then back down into my mouth. He moved his finger over and under my tongue, across my teeth, up inside my gums. Then he pushed another finger into my mouth and explored, pushing both fingers down my throat till I gagged. He pulled his fingers out and came closer. We looked into each others' eyes: his were filled with supercharged potential and wildness; mine were filled with all-devouring need.

"You have lips like wings," he said softly.

Then he kissed my lips like wings and the world cracked open, and I fell right into the void. *Sweet mother of Pearl. Sometimes, if you're lucky, you get just what you wish for.*

"Get in."

He opened the car door. I got in and waited for him to close the door, but he didn't. Instead he turned me so's my legs were hanging out, my feet touching the ground.

"Slide forward. Move that sweet ass towards me."

I did like he told me. When he saw that I wasn't wearing panties he growled.

"Open up."

I spread my legs.

"Not that much."

I un-spread them some.

He fell down onto his knees in front of me and stuck his head between my legs, inhaling deeply. He groaned. He ran his face along the inside of my thighs. He ran his tongue over the inside of my thighs. Then he stood, unzipped his pants, and exposed himself.

"You'd like this inside of you, wouldn't you?"

"Does a bear shit in the wood? Is the *atomic weight* of Cobalt fifty-eight point nine three three two?"

He laughed. I stared at Mister Happy. Hot muzzy juice oozed between my legs, moistening the leather beneath my backside.

"What did you say? I didn't hear you."

"I sure would."

"You've had others inside you?"

I started to count back from one hundred. He fell to his knees and ran his hands up the inside of my thighs.

"I didn't hear you."

I was just at eighty-nine but I figured "some" would about cover it, so that's what I said.

"Ever married?"

"Funny," I said.

"Children?"

I thought about how many times I'd been pregnant; I'd lost count. I thought about joking about how abortion was my preferred method of birth control, but, hey, why risk being a kill-joy?

"Very funny."

He inched closer to my hot biscuit.

"You like it in the mouth."

"Yessir."

"You've had others inside that mouth."

"Oh, yessir."

"You're a whore, a cocksucker?"

"I'm a whore and a cocksucker," I panted agreeably.

"Your sins, which are many, are about to be forgiven."

His fingers reached the Promised Land. *And away we go.*

"Oh, yeah," he growled and pulled my pussy lips open. "The first thing I'm going to put inside of you is this."

I strained to see. He held up his middle finger and then stuck it in his mouth.

"I'm going to fuck you with my finger first. I need to know you – inside and out. I need to know how deep I can go. How much you can take."

Oh, Daddy.

He finger-fucked me, slow, fast, hard, and tender.

"Now these."

I strained. He held up two fingers.

"Lean back," he ordered.

I let my head drop, wiping drool from my mouth. He fucked me real good with two fingers.

"Now look at me, Honey. Look at me as I move my fingers in and out of your sweet cunt. Look into my eyes. Look at my prick."

Oh, please, Br'er Fox, don't throw me into the briar patch.

"Ooh, baby, you're almost ready," he growled. "I do believe you can take it all."

"Oh, I can take it all, all right! Give it to me, Daddy!"

He threw his head back and laughed.

"Pretty soon I'm going to fuck you with this."

He rose slowly and stood in front of me, taking hold of Mister *Very* Happy.

"You're going to have to open up real wide for me. Wide open."

He massaged himself and smiled.

"Can you take it, good girl? Do you want it?"

I put my tongue out and panted like a dog.

"Tell me. Tell me all about it."

Words. He wants more fucking words. Fuck.

"Oh, I want it, all right," I said, struggling to catch my breath. "I can take it."

"Please?"

Beg for it? You-fucking-betcha.

"Please. Please. Please. Please."

"You're almost ready," he said and bent down between my legs again. "I want you to take your time. You have all the time in the world. This is all there is now. Me, fucking you. You, getting fucked."

Oh, Daddy.

He worked his fingers into me again and began to masterfully massage my hot spot with his other hand. And then, *yabba dabba do,* I gasped. This squirrely Casa-fucking-nova was about to perform a fucking miracle.

"Easy, baby," he said, sensing my impending O. "Take your time. There's no rush. I'm not going anywhere."

He moved his mouth down and started to gently lick, nibble, and suck my hardening rosebud. I went totally native, wildly gyrating and thrusting.

"Slow down."

"I can't. I'm . . . I'm . . . " I inhaled, and next thing I knew I was howling like a banshee as the mother of all orgasms surged through my body from the tips of my toes to the top of my head.

"Hold still. Hold still, baby. Let me feel you pulsing against me. Hold still. I've got you. Oh, yeah, that's right, good girl. Feel your power! Feel your strength!"

He held me still and firm, and my orgasm contracted and released, gripping his fingers like a vice in long and mighty spasms. And I thought, *Good gravy, this squirrely ole fella knows exactly what he's talking about: I am strong; I do have power.* And then something really screwy happened: I started to cry. I dropped my head back so's Creed wouldn't see my shame, and I stared up at the roof of the Javelin while my Big O slowly petered out and my body went limp.

Creed lifted me to sitting; he licked my tears. Still there was no pity in him. He moved closer. Major Packwood stood at attention, an inch from my mouth. Mercy, I was spent. But I owed Daddy: time to call on my inner cocksucker. I leaned forward. He pushed me back.

"On your belly," he growled.

I made the time-out sign with my hands, trying to catch a breath. He laughed and howled up at the moonless sky.

"There are no more time-outs!" He pushed me down and flipped me over and pulled me towards him. "Daddy's here!"

He pushed my skirt up and spread my legs. He rubbed my fleshy bazoo, massaged my cheeks, and snarled. Then he started to work my asshole. Licking, sucking, biting. Gentle and not so gentle. Then he worked my cheeks – spanking, kissing, licking. Again and again and again he worked on me, and I cried and laughed till I was beside myself. Then he reached into the backseat and brought out a black bag. I tried to get a better look, but he pushed me down and held me down with one hand.

"Trust me. I know what you need."

Who was I to argue? But suddenly a wave of intoxicating fear washed over my body. *What did he have in that black bag? A gun? A knife? Was he gonna hurt me? Cut me up?* But then another thought brought me to my senses: *Ah, hell, we've all gotta go sometime.*

"I'd never hurt you," he said, reading my mind.

I heard paper ripping, then the sound of rubber snapping. *Rubber gloves?* I heard what sounded like the unscrewing of a lid. *Astroglide Shooters?* I felt something cold and gooey on my starfish. My heart skipped a beat. This old fella wasn't just a cross-breed of Svengali and Casanova – a freakish spawn of fiction and nonfiction, evil hypnotist and the world's greatest lover – *he was a fucking proctologist!* – my *personal* proctologist! *Was this my lucky night or what?*

"That's a good girl. Relax. Open up. That's good. Oh, yeah. That's right. Open up for Daddy."

He pushed a finger up my dirt box. It slid in without resistance or pain – which was no great shocker, considering that having an enema nozzle shoved up my ass was about as regular an occurrence as the sun setting in the west.

He moved his finger in and out, then leaned forward – his body pressing down on me – till his mouth was close to my ear. His breathing was heavy.

"Oh, baby. You are wide open," he whispered.

I was something else, too. With my sense of sight totally subdued, my sense of sound had kicked into high gear. I felt like a bat, hyper-alert. Every little sound – natural or unnatural – made my yum-yum quiver and ooze.

"Ooooo, baby," he groaned, "you were born to be filled up. And I am the man who's going to do it." He pushed in deeper. "Can you feel yourself opening up, drinking me into you?"

"Oh, yes. I can feel myself opening up, all right!"

His sweat ran down my face.

"How many fingers?" I asked.

"One."

"How far in?"

"Up to the knuckle."

He added more of the cool lube and continued to work in and out, spreading me wider and wider.

"How many fingers?" I moaned.

"Three."

"How far in?"

"All the way."

He eased his fingers out of me and I heard some rustling. Then he ran his tongue down my back.

"Now I'm going to fuck your ass with *Daddy's little helper*," he chuckled.

I strained to see what he was pulling out of his bag of tricks. When I got a load of it I started to squirm. It wasn't little. He held me down.

"Don't worry," he laughed. "It's not as big as Daddy's, as you can see. But I have to get you ready for the real thing."

He ran his tongue over my asshole and then down into my muffin again. He growled.

"Gimme the real thing! I want the real thing! C'mon! *Please*. Fuck me, already!"

"Adopt the pace of nature," he said calmly. "Her secret is patience."

He continued to eat me out, rubbing his face back and forth. Then he stopped and spanked my bazoo, and then he shoved Daddy's not-so-little helper up my butthole. There was no opposition.

"You were made for this, baby."

He moved his other hand under my Mary Jane and rubbed and sucked my cherry pit and fucked me in the ass with the big hard dildo, and, *kow-abunga*: miracle number two.

In the middle of my O and before I could catch my breath, he dragged me outta the car and leaned me up against the door. My legs were so weak and wobbly that he had to hold me up. With his free hand he threw open his coat and took hold of his willy and started to rub it up and down, slowly.

"You want this."
I nodded, gasping for air. He waited for an answer.
"Yes," I said weakly, spit dribbling down the corners of my mouth.
He laughed madly.
"Let's take a drive."

Creed Kurgan was an accident waiting to happen. He only knew two positions on the gas and brake pedals: all the way down or all the way up. We raced in high-speed lurching jerks around the sharp curving desert roads to the lake, about six miles outta town. He didn't say a word, even when I jokingly observed – while holding on for dear life – that when he's on the road he must see more middle fingers than a manicurist.

■ ■ ■

The sky was black, the air cold as ice. Creed parked the Javelin near the edge of the lake and got out, motioning me to follow. I did. He took off his long black coat and laid it on the ground.
"Sit."
I sat, shivering.
"The car is heated."
I thought it was a perfectly reasonable suggestion, but I guess Creed didn't, cuz without a word he took off his clothes and walked right into the big black loch, immersing himself below the surface and reemerging like a geyser with a suggestion of his own.
"Come in."
"No thanks. I'm already colder than a well digger's ass." I laughed and hugged my quivering knees.
He came outta the water and sat next to me.
"I dare you," he ragged.
I pulled my eyes away from his pecker – which, incredibly, was still fucking hard – and looked at the water.
"I dare you," he said again.
"You *dare* me?"
"Yes, Honey McGuinness. I *dare* you."

Fuck. I was just about dumb enough to take him up on it. In fact, I *was* dumb enough. I stood and my bum leg gimped up and I clumsily removed my clothes, trying not to fall flat on my can. And then, as if it wasn't bad enough that I was gonna go into the fucking ice-cold water on a dare, I found myself standing stark naked in front of Daddy. Now, you'd think that after all that had happened between us – the s-e-x and such – a gal like me wouldn't be bothered by being in the altogether in front of a fella, but you'd be wrong. I never could get comfortable in my body. Never felt beautiful. Fact is, in all my past years of flesh-on-flesh, I'd never stood naked in front of a fella. Not once. But that was then and this was now. I held my breath and let my arms dangle so's they covered my cha-cha. Creed stared intently.

"You can't hide from me. I know everything there is to know about you. I know who you are – not who they made you think you were – but who you *really* are. All those impotent, egotistical weaklings . . . all they can see is their own reflections. But they're blind . . . the blind leading the blind," he scoffed. "What they think they see doesn't even exist! They could *never* recognize a woman like you. You're different. You're a misfit. A loner. You're an orphan, without family, without friends. You're an outsider. Tell me I'm wrong."

I couldn't.

"Of course I'm right. I know; I'm the same. People like you and me, we don't play by their rules. We make our own rules. We see things differently. What they call sin, we call pleasure. What they call truth, we call lies. I know you, Honey McGuinness. I know you never felt safe in the world. I know you never had a chance. And I know I'm the man who's going to change all of that. Do you believe me?"

"Au reservoir." I turned and hobbled slowly into the icy water, unable to tell him I did.

"A drawing starts with a blank piece of paper. A tall tree grows from a tiny sprout," he shouted. "A nine-story tower rises from a heap of earth. And you . . . you, woman, are a blank canvas, the mother of everything – the origin—"

He kept talking, but I couldn't make out the words cuz I was having some kinda brain freeze, even though I wasn't but waist deep.

"OK. I did it!" I hollered.

"That's not *in*. Swim out. Unless you don't *dare*," he shouted back.

He sure did have my number. I grumbled, but bit the bullet. I dog-paddled out to the middle of the lake, then turned around and dog-paddled back. I tried to stand and walk in the shallow water but I was shaking something fierce, so's I crawled ashore.

"Cold enough?"

"Cold enough to freeze the balls off a brass monkey," I said through quavering nippers.

He laughed softly, picked up our clothes, took my hand, and led me to a spot under a pine tree. He bent down and scooped together a pile of needles.

"Sit."

I did like he said. Then he sat, with his back against mine.

"Now give me your arms."

I reached back and he intertwined his arms with mine. And there we sat, back to back, in the freezing winter night.

"You'll never be cold again."

The heat of his body started to replace my coldness. Soon I felt hot, solid – part of the earth and the night – part of the man in the long black coat. Abruptly, he stood and ran behind a tree.

"One thousand one, one thousand two . . ." he counted.

I laughed and loped best I could, stark-bone-naked, into the forest. I felt wild as a young filly, stripped of all weight, free of all burden. I felt new, reborn, unscarred and unmaimed.

"You can run, but you can't hide," he warned.

He caught me easily and pulled me down onto my back. He laughed and growled and picked my legs up and scooched in between them. He took hold of his still-hard bozack and started to rub it very slowly back and forth against my girlfriend. He pushed in ever so slightly – but didn't enter me. I was slavering.

"What does a gal have to do around here to get fucked?"

He smiled and drew me up to him and wrapped his arms around me and said something about "being clean." Then he pushed me back down and lay next to me. He put my hand around his woody and I held on tightly. He pulled my head to his chest.

"Listen closely, Honey. What do you hear? Do you hear it? Your name. My heart is beating out your name. My heart is beating only for you."

He stuck his finger inside my poon. I couldn't hear his heart beating out my name, but I pressed my head against his chest and listened anyways, cuz right about then I would've done anything he told me to do.

I woke up whistling Dixie. I wouldn't say I was feeling particularly "good." It was something more complicated. I was feeling kinda freakish, like I'd been part of a harebrained lab experiment gone haywire. Every cell in my body felt tuned and ready to roll. My forehead was so hot you could fry an egg on it. My asshole was the size of a silver dollar.

I wondered: *Why hadn't he given up the gravy? Why had he fucked me with everything* but *Big Jim?* Not that I was complaining. I mean, beggars can't be choosers. And just thinking about how he'd prepared for the *"experiment"* – with his black bag, his rubber gloves, his cool lube, his big black dildo – well, it made me hot in the biscuit all over again.

I began to fondle myself. I pictured Creed going from store to store – attentively searching the shelves for each special *item* – selecting just the right one – the one with my name on it. I thought about how he knew he was gonna use these items on *me* – how he calculated the whole thing. Then I thought about how he said he would've come sooner but he knew I'd "take some time." And just like that, *pay dirt*.

I was hungry as a bear. But I'd have to settle for the ole Mexican break-fast: water and a cigarette, if I could find one. I rolled outta bed but could hardly walk. Besides being gimp, I was as bowlegged as a wishbone, my knees wanting to go in opposite directions. My movements were spastic and gawky, but I managed to find a small butt on the floor. I poured myself a glass of water and sat down at the small kitchen table.

How had I gotten home last night? I couldn't remember a thing. Maybe I had passed out. Maybe Creed had had to call a doctor.

"You'd better sit down for this," says the doctor gravely, after examining me. "That bad, doc?" I ask. He nods somberly and says, "Afraid so." "Tell me, doc. Give it to me straight. I can take it," I say. "It's . . . it's . . ." It's so bad he can't even say the words. "C'mon, doc, spill." The doc takes a deep breath and spills, "It's D.O.O." "Oh, no!" I say, "not Dreaded Orgasmic Overload!"

I laughed. The diagnosis would've been just about right. I mean, I was the sex-starved gal who couldn't even go it alone anymore. And when it came to giving it up to others . . . well, the last time that happened was in a mucky urine-filled alley when I paid a toothless junkie named CeCe ten bucks to eat my buju – and don't you know, she pulled it off, though I had to suffer a blistering dressing-down cuz I said "Oh, baby, you're so good" just like one of her other "typical jizz-ass johns." Yeah, that was me . . . then. But not anymore! Things were different now. Now, thanks to some greasy ole clitoromaniac, I was a fucking multi-orgasm machine! I licked my lips. *Mmm, mmm, good.* Oh yeah, I'd been fucked – inside and out. And I'll be a monkey's uncle if there was a gal alive who didn't need it more than me.

Yep, it was a brand-new day! The flesh-ache was gone. The psycho-meter had plummeted. I felt light as a feather – hopeful, even. *Funny how some first-class hanky-panky can make a gal forget her woes.* Having had my fill of s-e-x, I figured I could maybe pick up right where I'd left off . . . crack this "normalcy" nut once and for all. *Why not?* After all, before I became a sex-crazed horn-dog I was really starting to get somewhere.

"Why, Romeo," Alice said to mini-mutt, "I do believe our girlfriend is wearing *lipstick*!"

I placed a cup of joe on the table and looked around, my face all colored up. Lucky Frank tipped his Stetson and gave me the wink-wink. Maggie screwed up her forehead – maybe wondering if she'd made a big mistake by forgiving my "transgression" and giving me a second chance after I promised to lay off the juice. Dunk Hayward raised his beer and his eyebrows. Fob Johnson looked over his glasses. Mr. Stick-in-the-mud Buddy Pinchback paid me no never-mind. Romeo gave a little yip.

"Eat my shorts," I muttered softly under my breath and stepped back behind the bar.

"Just sayin'..." Alice laughed.

I flipped her the bird, which quickly turned into a "howdy-do" gesture as a posse of local cowmen piled through the door. They ordered Pie Slicers and bull burgers.

"Sorry, gentlemen, we're all out of bull," Maggie said.

"But we've got all the bullshit you can eat," I added.

This got hoots and hollers all around; Alice laughed so's water sprayed right outta her nose; even Punchclock couldn't stifle a couple of yuks – which must've just about killed the manhole.

Alice was right. I *was* wearing lipstick, come-hither red. I was also wearing a crinkled white pleated skirt and a big ole black sweater – both of which I'd drug out from the bottom of a pile of dirty clothes that hadn't seen daylight in a good long while. Instead of tucking my hair up under a baseball cap, I let it fall down my back in a long braid fastened by an elastic band with two red crystal balls at the end. I had a twinkle in my eyes and a bounce in my bazoo. All in all, I was feeling kinda . . . kittenish. *Meow.*

After work I whistled out from behind the bar and plopped down next to Alice and Romeo, who, like usual, were waiting on me to get off shift so we could go do our errands together.

Alice tilted her head, a big fat you've-been-up-to-something-and-I'm-gonna-find-out-what-it-is look on her face.

"What?" I asked, like I didn't know.

"You know what I want to know," she laughed.

"Hey, what I wanna know is what happened to my pal Alice. You know, the polite one, who doesn't butt into my business."

"Who is he?" she asked, ignoring me.

"He who?"

"I'll tell you what, Honey. It may be a coon's age since I've had any . . . *familiarity* in that particular area – and you know exactly what I mean by that – but I haven't forgotten what the morning after looks like. And it looks like red lipstick, and a silk skirt, and—"

"Knock it off, Alice," I said, trying to sound serious.

"Oh, c'mon, now. Tell me who he is!"

She gave me her sad, pleading face.

"You dating someone?" Maggie said, joining us at the table.

"Couldn't be someone from around these parts. We'd know about it. Wouldn't we, Romeo?" The pint-sized hound gave Alice a lick on the mouth.

"Well, whoever he is, I hope he's a God-fearing man. There's nothing as good as a God-fearing man," Maggie added.

I rolled my eyes.

"I'm sure Minister Stryker would agree with you on that, Maggie," Alice said with a consoling smile.

"Oh, Benezer would definitely agree. I'm sure he'd . . ."

They carried on about the minister like he was a saint, and I tuned out. Talking about preachers was a hot topic in Pie Town. Maybe that's cuz there were four churches in town. Being that the town was so small you had to leave it just to turn around, and being that the population was so teeny, well, that gave Pie Town the distinction of having more churches per capita than any place in the country. I'd met all the preachers in town, of course. E. Benezer Stryker was by far the biggest frog in the small pond. He ministered at Main Street Church, which, other than Sunday services – which I attended only cuz Alice attended – was busy with programs for the town kids every night of the week. Fact, the way the kids hung on him, well, it made me think predictably awful thoughts. But then again, I only thought those thoughts cuz I was another all-Catholic-priests-must-be-pedophiles dumb-ass hose-bag. Anyways.

I gave Alice the time-out sign. I wasn't gonna tell anyone about Creed. He was *my* secret, *my* mystery, *my* lover. And I intended to keep it that way.

"So, how about them Yankees?" I said with a big smile.

Alice looked miserable; she wasn't gonna get the skinny. Maggie looked kinda relieved.

"Oh, heck. All right," Alice shrugged. "Let's give Maggie some peace and quiet. C'mon, Honey, we've got errands to run. First, the post office." She smiled cagily. "Big news!" She paused for effect. "From my boys! They're coming home!"

"Really? Now that's some news—"

"I wouldn't hold my breath if I were you," Maggie interrupted harshly.

"Well, I'm not you, Maggie Horton! And whether you believe it or not doesn't much matter." Alice turned to me. "Oh, Honey, wait till you meet the boys! They're the spitting image of each other. The only way you can tell Clyde from Clovis is by a little indentation in his forehead." She pointed to a spot above her temple. "Clyde didn't come out as willingly as Clovis," she explained. "The doctor had to use forceps, of all things!"

"Well, like I said, I wouldn't hold my breath," Maggie repeated.

I gave Maggie a quick, cutting look, then smiled at Alice.

"How do you know they're coming?"

"They wrote me a letter."

"Is that right?" I said, my mind wandering to the letter I'd seen on the counter in the motel office.

"What?" Alice asked. "Is something wrong?"

"Oh, it's probably nothing. But, well, I saw that letter. And, well, I was meaning to say something about the postmark. I mean—"

"Oh, don't go causing any more trouble, Honey!" Maggie said, hitting her fist on the table. "That's just nonsense!"

How did she know it was nonsense?

"It's all right, Maggie. Honey has something to say, I want to hear it." Alice looked at me searchingly. "What about it?"

"Well, it was kinda . . . I don't know . . . *funny.*"

"Funny how?"

"I can't explain it. Let's go to the post office. I'll show you what I mean."

Me and Alice and Romeo headed out and Maggie, still flustered and worked up, flipped the sign on the door to "Closed."

"That's weird," I said. "Maggie never closes shop while the sun's still shining."

Alice shrugged and pulled my arm.

"Oh, don't bother about Maggie. She'll be all right."

"Well, she sure was encouraging about your boys coming to see you."

"Don't be hard on her." She stopped me and said in a low voice, like there was someone who might hear us, "The poor thing can't have children. Wanted them desperately. But God had another plan for her, I guess. So, you know, she's a little touchy on the subject. I don't take it personally."

"You're a bigger woman than me, Alice Guthrie!"

"Ain't that the truth!" she hooted, then put me in an arm-lock and pulled me along. "Hey, did I ever tell you about my list?" She didn't wait for an answer. "No? Well, there are five things on my list – five things that I love more than anything in the world. Know what they are? Well, first there's tissues. You know, Kleenex tissues. The soft kind. I love tissues. Second, I love quarters. Not pennies, not nickels, not dimes, just quarters. They're the perfect size and the perfect weight. They're just perfectly perfect. Third thing is my little man, of course." She patted Romeo's pin-head. "Fourth, my twins – even if they were a handful, and even if they did run off and leave their mama to run the motel all by herself. And the fifth thing, well, can you guess?" She smiled broadly. "Guess, Honey! What's the fifth thing on my list?"

I couldn't answer cuz I wasn't paying attention to the first four things on her list cuz pictures of Daddy kept flashing across my mind. But I stopped and took a good long look at this big gal with her little mutt. I sure did like Alice, and I wanted to remember this moment: I was afraid we might not be running too many more errands together.

"You, Honey! You're the fifth thing on my list!"

I was touched, I really was. But at the same time I felt kinda lousy cuz I didn't have a list, and if perfectly normal Alice had one, well, that meant every other gal in Pie Town had one too and that meant . . . and then it hit me.

"Nice try, Alice! You think you can butter me up and I'm gonna tell you whether or not I've got a fella? Forget it. You're wasting your time. There's nothing to tell. And even if there was, wild horses couldn't drag it outta me."

"Why, I don't have the slightest idea what you're talking about," she said sheepishly.

"Give it a rest."

We walked on. I was hoping for a little quiet so's I could think about Daddy, but Alice kept baby-talking to Romeo. She never could appreciate a moment's worth of silence.

Buddy Pinchback wasn't happy to see me. Some things never change. But he was cordial enough to Alice.

"Can I have my mail, please, Buddy?"

"Sorry. You don't have any."

"But I'm expecting a letter."

"You don't have one."

"Check again, Punchclock," I demanded.

He gave me a dirty look and grumbled, but he went to check again. We waited. And waited. And waited. Finally I shouted, "He couldn't go any slower if he was molasses going uphill," and picked up the latest edition of *The Fourth Wave*. "What a bunch of baloney," I said, showing it to Alice.

"To each his own, that's what I say."

I shrugged, then pointed to the "Pie Town, Pop. 86" printed on the front. I made a sad face.

"Hey now," she said sympathetically, "you'll always be number 87 in my book." She gave me a soft pat on the back. "You just keep your pecker up."

"It ain't over till it's over," I said.

"That's the spirit!"

Alice sure was a sweet gal.

After forever Buddy returned.

"Like I said, no mail."

Alice was visibly heartbroken.

"Don't worry." It was my turn to do some consoling and gentle back patting. "It'll be here tomorrow, won't it, Punchclock?"

"I told you, don't call me that," he snarled.

"You going to Springerville tomorrow, or wherever it is you go to pick up the mail?"

He ignored my question.

"You know, I was just about to tell Alice here about that funny-looking postmark. You know what I'm talking about, dontcha, Punch—"

"I warned you twice already. I won't warn you again."

Before things got ugly, Alice dragged me outside.

"Seems I'm always rubbing that doober's fur the wrong way."

"Oh, Buddy's harmless enough." Alice raised her eyebrows. "Just not too crazy about girls, if you know what I mean."

"*Punchclock?*"

"Queer as a three-dollar bill."

"Well, stick a fork in me, I'm done."

Alice laughed and slapped her thigh and told me I was a pisser. As we crossed the interstate, Alice said, "Now, tell me about the postmark," and I did.

■ ■ ■

I was in Room #5 giving myself a much-needed shower and thinking about Daddy and just about to give my genital area a good scrubbing when Alice burst through the door and yanked the shower curtain open.

"*What the f—*"

"They're gone!"

"Who's gone?"

"The letters! The letters from my boys! They're gone!"

Pop and Josie Clover couldn't find the letter they got from Daisy. Pop thought it might've found its way into the garbage – which just about broke Josie's heart. When we got to Caudill Jackson's place he said he'd only gotten two, maybe three letters from Goose. He said the boy had been gone over a year, but didn't write much. After Mrs. Jackson died, he and the boy had started to "butt heads." "Spare the rod, spoil the child," he added, with a fearsome gaze. We asked him if he could look for the letters. He went to collect them. He thought they were maybe on his nightstand. He came back empty-handed.

Alice, trembling and hugging Romeo tight against her bazongas, delivered the "shocking" news: her letters had been stolen too. The reaction from Caudill Jackson was the same as it had been from the Clover's when we went back to deliver the news: a big heap of cynicism. Both times Alice looked to me to remove their doubt.

"Tell them, Honey," she'd said. "Tell them about the postmark!"

I could've kicked myself for starting the whole rigmarole. Especially cuz about an hour before Alice dragged me outta the shower and into the cold, half-naked, I suffered a rapid vertical nosedive – mentally and physically speaking. And I started to feel totally empty again; in need of filling up. And by the time we got to the Clover place I was obsessing something awful, a constant loop of questions fueling my phobia. *Where was Daddy? Why didn't he come to see me? Didn't he want me? When would I see him again? Would I see him again? Who the fuck was he?* Plus, the fact that I had the shakes from giving up the juice cold-turkey just made me more jumpy and discomfited. Yeah. I was big-time distracted. And all that being so, I started to see the whole "postmark" situation in a totally different light. I mean, Maggie was right: I was just a big-city gal looking for some small-town trouble; it was all a bunch of hooey. I mean, who the fuck would steal *anyone's* letters? No one, that's who. Plain and simple: Daisy Clover's letter had been thrown out. Pop Clover admitted as much; Caudill Jackson, well, he might've done the same, seeing as how he seemed to get some kind of sadistic pleasure from recalling how he gave Goose the what-for; and as for Alice, she'd most likely misplaced them, messy as she was. And the funny-looking postmark? Well, that could easily be explained by Buddy Pinchback . . . to someone without knockers. Anyways, over Alice's displeasure, that's the line I sold Jackson and the Clovers, and that's the line they bought.

■ ■ ■

Two days later Alice was still looking for those damn letters. Two days later Daddy still hadn't come around. And two days later I was still sober, but slowly coming unhinged. I tried not to think about Creed; I tried to go about my business, like I had before I met him. At noon I thought I saw the Javelin speed past the El Serape. By the time I got out from behind the bar alls I could see was a dark speck disappearing down I-60 towards Route 6.

Three days later I felt sick and piteous. I gave up trying not to think about Creed. Every bone in my body hurt for wanting him so bad. *I had to have him. I had to.* It was worse than the crack-ache I'd had back on the Row. The Row! Skinner P. Ochs! *Why didn't I think of that sooner?* Sure, thinking about Skinner always worked: he was my fantasy man, my dream lover, my trusted diversion, my obsession. But it didn't work. Skinner had been replaced . . . by Creed. I tried my ever faithful friend, the enema bag. Bupkis. Nothing but Daddy was gonna bring me relief. *Mofo, this was bad.*

■ ■ ■

I blew Alice off. She had become a real fucking thorn in my bohunkus – constantly pestering me about her missing fucking letters or this or that. And I blew off work. I puked all day Saturday and into the night. Around eleven o'clock I gave. Sobriety was for the birds.

48

I rifled around the trailer, but I was outta luck: no scratch. *Fuck.* Then I looked across the room, and there it was – the little cardboard box with Mike McGuinness's thin black billfold and forty-five smackeroos. *Hot diggity dog . . . finally, Father provides!*

I went to Anita's and bought a fifth of her best rot-gut. Maybe a large quantity of the Devil's brew would give me a brand-new outlook on life. I sure did need one.

As I approached my trailer I noticed that someone had done a little redecorating in my absence. GO HOME SLUT was sprayed across the side in big black letters. *How thoughtful.* I touched the surface: still wet. I went inside and swilled the forty-rod till it was all gone. It took the edge off my shakes, but other than that it didn't help. I threw the dead dog across the room; it hit the mirror. I stared at the shattered pieces. Things had gone from bad to worse. The obsessive Daddy loop now included new thoughts and questions: *Lucky Frank was so close-mouthed that you'd have to pry open his lips with a crowbar before he'd tattletale. So, if it wasn't him – and I knew it wasn't – who else in town knew I was a slut?* and *where did that person think I was gonna go?* I mean, I *was* home.

To get things under control I started to count -- words . . . the number of letters in a word . . . the number of letters in a sentence – on my fingers. If they worked out in five or multiples of five: peace and calm. If they didn't: helter-skelter.

Words like CREED, HONEY, DEATH, INTOXICATE – they were good. Words like SKINNER, LOVE, HATE, ASSHOLE – they were bad. Sentences like "NOW I BELONG TO YOU" were very good. Sentences like "DO WITH ME WHAT YOU WILL" were very bad. When I counted out the very good sentence "SHORT TIGHT DRESS" I decided to put one on. I also pulled on my black velvet ankle-strapped high heels. Then I put on a thick coating of red lipstick and staggered back to Anita's.

■ ■ ■

"We're out of Ring Dings."

"I don't want Ring Dings."

"You won't be getting more whiskey."

"I don't want whiskey."

I leaned against the counter. She waved away the smell of booze on my breath and gave me the ole leather-eye.

"You sell spray paint?"

"Not to huffers, I don't."

"I don't want to sniff it." I snickered at her ridiculous suggestion. But wait a sec. *Maybe it wasn't so ridiculous. I mean, I could be huffer.* The thought sent my mind into a hullabaloo. Suddenly I couldn't remember where I was or what I was doing and I was seeing two of everything, including the formidable Pueblo Indian standing in front of me with arms folded. She could out-wait Job. Then it all came back.

"I've got it, Watson! I want to know if you sold any spray paint lately. Black spray paint."

She nodded.

"To who?"

"Rabbit."

"Rabbit Rawlings?"

Rabbit Rawlings was a sixteen-year old albino – straight-A student, altar boy, sweet kid.

"You know any other Rabbit?"

■ ■ ■

I found Rabbit Rawlings coming out of Main Street Church. I grabbed him by the scruff of his neck and dragged him around back. I might've been pie-eyed and wobbly, but I could still take a timid, skinny teenager.

"So you think I'm a slut?"

"What?"

I knocked his head against the wall.

"Keep your voice down, Rabbit. You understand?"

He nodded.

"Where have you been?"

"Bible class."

I knocked his head against the wall.

"Bible class, I swear!"

"You bought spray paint. From Anita."

He started to whimper.

"What for?"

He didn't answer. I knocked his head against the wall. He started to blubber.

"*What for?*"

"Detailing."

"Detailing the side of my trailer? With a nasty four-letter word?"

When he didn't answer quick enough, I knocked his head against the wall again.

"Ouch!" he rubbed the back of his head. "I wasn't detailing any trailer. It was for my friend's car, that's all."

"I don't like liars."

"I swear it's true."

"God doesn't like liars."

"I . . . I'm not lying."

I stared into his little pink albino eyes. He didn't look like a liar. I let him go and he went off, hippity-hop. I stumbled out to the road. I was all dressed up with somewhere to go.

■ ■ ■

The crowd was thin. I splurged on a Pig Nose, straight up. Before I could take a swig, Maggie showed up.

"Well, *Hellooooooo Dolly*," I sang. "Sorry I missed work again, but—"

"You won't be missing work anymore, Missy," she said, real unfriendly-like.

"I won't?" I slurred.

"No. You're fired. Tommy told me to tell you."

"Now why would he go and do a thing like that?" I slobbered.

"Tommy told me to tell you that he can't rely on you to show up for work anymore."

"Where is this *Tommy*? I don't believe there *is* a *Tommy*. I wanna talk to him!"

I tried to get off the stool, but my leg gimped up. I sat back down.

"You'd best get home," she said, cold as ice.

"Did *Tommy* tell you to tell me that, Missus *I-Can't-Think-Or-Speak-For-Myself?*"

I threw back my drink in one gulp, shivered as it went down, and slammed two sawbucks down on the bar. Then I ordered a second.

"Well, seeing as how I'm a cash-paying hophead . . ." I threw back the second drink and ordered a third. ". . . you can tell your *Tommy* that he can't fire me . . . cuz I quit! Work is interfering with my drinking!"

She got redder than a gander in a huckleberry patch and stormed off in a huff.

"Smell ya later, Magpie," I said, holding up my glass.

Two sawbucks' worth of Pig Nose later the bar was crowded. Lucky Frank ambled in and tipped his hat. I smiled sweetly. Then I threw back my last shot and stumbled outside.

I took the Winchester from the rack in Lucky Frank's pick-up truck and grabbed some extra bullets from the glove box. Lucky Frank had offered to take me shooting a couple of times. He said he could pick twenty cans off a fence using twenty bullets, at a distance of some forty-five yards. He told me I could do the same – said it was easy. I was about to find out.

I stumbled back into the bar and stood at the door.

"*Is everybody happy?*" I shouted in my best oom-pa-pa accent, and waved the rifle over my head.

No one seemed happy. I cocked the gun and pointed randomly. Bodies went flying – ducking for cover.

"*Ah-one,*" I said, and took aim at the stuffed big horn head mounted on the wall across the room. I pulled the trigger. Missed. "*Ah-two,*" I said, and shot at the stuffed mule deer head mounted on the wall behind the register. Missed. "*Ah-three,*" I said, and took aim at the stuffed buffalo head mounted on the wall above. . . .

. . . *Hey, just a minute, buster! Was I seeing right? Was that really Buddy Wannabe-A-Fudge-Packer Pinchback sitting there about to stuff a spoonful of pie into his yap, like I wasn't standing here pointing a loaded rifle in his direction? Well, I'll be a suck-egg mule!*

I pulled the trigger once, twice, three times. I hit the poor buffalo right between the eyes. The beast quivered like he was about to rise from the dead. And then – in slo mo – the humongous head wrenched loose from the wall and fell . . . right on top of Punchclock's noodle.

There was only one sure way I knew to prevent a hangover: stay drunk. Now, of course, staying liquored-up would require some liquor . . . which I didn't have. What I did have was a toe-curling head-pounding and a killer case of the queasies. While I made bahli-bahli for the crapper – hoping to avoid another barf fest on my tight little mini-dress – I noticed two things: Bullwinkle was dangling from the wall by a thread, victim of some inconsiderate moose-hater who put her last bullet right through his unrecognizable body; and Lucky Frank's Winchester was lying in the middle of the floor.

Fifteen minutes of dry heaves, ten minutes of O.C.D. counting – *motherfucker*: twelve letters; very, very bad; *inconsiderate motherfucker*: five multiples of five letters; very, very good – and one cigarette butt later, I was up and out the door of my trailer.

■ ■ ■

"Some people knock," Alice said sarcastically.

"Shh, shh, shh." I put my hand up. "I've got a twenty-inch double-foot bass banging on my auditory cortex." It actually hurt to talk.

She banged the medicine cabinet open and shut a few times to let me know how sympathetic she wasn't.

"Come to Mama," she said, and picked Romeo up and set him on the counter. Then she went about the business of putting on her face for church – acting like I wasn't sitting on the john, right there next to her, with a hangover the size of Texas.

I lit a smoke, patted Romeo on his noodle, and said, "Nice doggie," hoping to score a couple of points. But Alice continued the cold-shoulder treatment, and the pint-sized cur cowered and growled, like he did every time I tried to pat his rotten little pinhead.

"I thought I was on your list," I whispered, blowing smoke at the little fucker.

She waved the smoke out of Romeo's face. "Yeah, well, lists can be rewritten!" She picked up an eyelash curler and moved closer to the mirror.

"I thought we were pals."

"The word "pals" implies a two-way street!" She set the eyelash curler down and started applying thick black mascara.

"Can you just talk a little softer?" I asked, rubbing my temples.

"I rescued you from the side of the road!" she yelled, answering my question. "I carried your boxes! I brought you into town! I took you in! I vouched for you with *my* friends – Maggie and Lucky Frank, both! Without me you wouldn't have a place to live or a job! You'd probably *still* be standing on the side of the road!" She set down the mascara and picked up the eyelash curler again. "And what's on your side of the street, *pal*? Oh, gee, let me think. Oh, right. A pal who tells me something's fishy about letters from my boys – *letters that just happen to mean the whole world to me, in case anybody cared!* – then says, *Oops, just kidding*, so that I'm the one who ends up looking like a total nut job in front of *my* friends! A pal who doesn't even give me the time of day anymore, because, why? Oh, gee, let me see why." She swapped the curler for the mascara. "Why? Because she's too drunk! Why? Oh, let me see why. Oh, right! Because she's turned into a lousy alky-stiff! Oh yeah, and there's one more thing. What could it be? Hmm. Oh, right! A pal who plays shoot 'em up with *real bullets* – shooting at *my* friends – like she's living in the Wild Wild West!" She looked at me for a brief second, then turned back to the mirror. "*You* may not care what other people think, but I do. And I'll be living here long after *you're* gone!" She switched the mascara for the curler again.

Did she have to talk so loud?

"I'm not going anywhere," I whispered, then added, "Besides, a gal's gotta be accorded a little wild now and then."

"You hear that, Romeo?" She patted his tiny noodle. "She calls *that* a little wild!"

"I guess you heard I lost my job," I sighed, fishing for a little sympathy. Bupkis. "I lost my job for no good reason." She rolled her eyes, like there was plenty good reason. "Yeah, well, fuck Tommy."

She turned and waggled her eyelash curler a quarter-inch from my face. "You watch your mouth, Honey McGuinness! Don't be going around badmouthing people who can't defend themselves. Tommy has suffered enough, and so has Maggie. She takes care of her husband like he was her very own baby – washes him, feeds him, dresses him. Why, he hasn't been out of that apartment since he fell down the stairs – going on . . . ten years, maybe more. I can't even remember, it's been so long. The Hortons are good, God-fearing people. They've had a hard life, and the last thing they need is *you* adding to their misery. *Shame on you!*"

I looked up and blinked once and gave her my Irresistible Smile, which, judging by her reaction, was gonna have to be renamed. I flicked a couple of chunks of stinky dried puke off my dress.

"Pee-u to high heaven!" she said, stating the obvious – which was why I came by Alice's in the first place: to get the key so's I could wash myself off.

"You're right, Alice. I should have *shame on me*, and don't think I don't." I hung my aching head in shame to prove that I did. Alice made a clucking sound. "Yes, I do. As a matter of fact, just this morning, before I came here, I dragged my putrid behind right over to the El Serape to tell Maggie just how much shame I had on me. I knocked and kicked and hollered, but she didn't even have the good manners to come down. So, don't you know, I stood right out there in the open with my tail between my legs and begged for her mercy and I said I'd work off the damages, if she and Tommy would just give me another chance. And you know what she did?" I snuffed my cigarette out in the sink and lit another. "That God-fearing-forgive-the-sinner do-right opened the window, stuck her flimflam head out, and shouted down, 'Tommy says you're *un-Christian*. He says you're out of chances. He says you're not welcome around here anymore.' Then she slams the window shut. Just like that." I took a big drag then exhaled. "So, how do you like them apples?"

She rolled her eyes and went on primping.

"Well, you know what I said?" I continued. Alice covered Romeo's ears, like she had to protect him from my foul mouth. "I said, 'Well, that's a cryin' shame, Maggie.'"

"Yeah? You're just lucky you didn't lose more than a job!"

"Umm."

"They should lock you up and throw away the key!"

"Someone payin' you to be judge and jury?"

"You go ahead, be a wisecracker. But you're about to lose the only friend you've got left in this town. Think about *that*!"

I thought about it.

"I guess you have a point."

"She *guesses*!" she said to Romeo, then to me, "You *guess*? Lord knows the only reason you're not in jail this very minute is that Dunk Hayward has a 'What happens in Pie Town, stays in Pie Town' type attitude – which you couldn't rightly say about most United States marshals! By the time he got over to the El Serape last night, you were gone. He didn't know where you were off to and he wasn't about to go chasing his tail around, so he called me – woke me up in the middle of the night, I might add, as if anybody cares! – and told me what happened and asked me to check the trailer. So me and my little man," she patted her little man's head, "had to traipse all the way out there in the dark of night, and we stood out there in the cold banging and banging, but, of course, you didn't answer the door. So we had to peek in the window – like Peeping Toms, for heaven's sake! And there you were – dead drunk!" She took a breath and applied bright orange lipstick. "So, I told Dunk you were out of the troublemaking business for the night." She blotted her lips on a tissue. "You were lucky last night. I saved your butt, again!" She pouted and gave her lips the once over and scowled in dissatisfaction. "But you know, Honey," she applied another coat of lipstick, "there's only one sure thing about luck."

"What's that?"

"It runs out."

I cocked my head. *What was she getting at?* I pressed my thumbs into my temples. *Think. Think. What happened last night? What did I do that was so bad?*

She looked at me with disgust and said, "Buddy?"

Suddenly, it all flashed before me like a bad B-movie.

"*Punchclock*. Fuck." I said softly. "*Did I? Is he—?*"

"No, he's not dead. Not yet!"

Did I detect a stifled smile?

"But he's in Springerville Hospital, in a coma."

I shook my head and said, "Talk about tough luck."

Her almost-smile almost cracked. But she quickly pulled herself together, harrumphed, dropped the lipstick into her pocketbook, snapped it shut, and picked Romeo up. She turned towards me.

"You've made enemies."

I nodded and said, "You can include one albino teenager on that list." Alice frowned. "Rabbit," I explained. "He decided to do a little advertising on the side of my trailer: GO HOME SLUT. Nice, big black letters. Guess you couldn't see it last night in the dark."

"Rabbit Rawlings? Don't be ridiculous! I'm knowing that boy his entire life. He'd *never* do something like that! Never!"

"Never is a long time. And sooner than later I'm gonna make sure that little cottontail faces the music."

"That's crazy talk! Probably all that booze sloshing around in your empty head! Playing tricks with your mind! Besides, words will wash off. You've got worse problems. People are all over Dunk to arrest you. And Dunk . . . well, he doesn't much like being told what to do, but he's up for re-election next year, and believe you me, he's not about to start a new career after thirty years just to save your skinny behind!"

She looked at me. I rubbed my head. She shook hers.

"Don't you get it?" she hollered so's I thought my head would pop. "*He could arrest you for attempted murder!*"

"No fooling?"

"They're just waiting for Buddy to press charges!"

I snuffed out one Newport and lit another.

"Could be waiting a long time . . . being as how he's unconscious and all."

Alice choked back a chortle, composed herself real quick, and marched off down the hall, with me in tow.

"I sure do hope Lucky Frank's ass isn't wound as tight as some folk," I said.

She stopped, swung around, looked me in the eyes, and made a face.

"What?"

"You're kidding, right? You used his rifle – you *stole* his rifle – to commit a crime!"

That fucker! And to think, he let me fuck him!

"Well, don't you worry about me," I said, hoping she would.

Her silence said she wouldn't. I trailed after her into the bedroom. She sat on the edge of the bed and struggled over her lumpy body to get into her pink polka dot pumps. The look was complete: in a Tammy Faye look-alike contest, she'd be the gal to beat.

"Maybe *I* oughta go to church," I said, hoping for any sign of clemency.

She stood up and checked herself in the mirror one last time. She nod-ded, satisfied.

"It's a free country," she said coldly.

I sure was gonna miss big ole Alice. *Alice*: five letters; good.

I grabbed the key to Room #5. *Number five*: two sets of five, ten letters; good. I had every intention of going to Room #5 and maybe even going to church, but the thing was that in order to get there, I had to walk right through Alice's kitchen. And when I walked through Alice's kitchen, well, there he was: Jose Cuervo. *Jose Cuervo*: two sets of five, ten letters; good. Very, very good, cuz as a matter of fact I sure did need a little hair of the dog.

I skipped the shower and headed for home, saying *Hola, amigo* to Jose as I crossed the butte. As I approached I thought, *Now isn't that special,* cuz the touching message on the trailer had been abbreviated a smidge. Now it read: O ME SLUT. Someone had tried to scratch off the paint; in the process they'd dinged up the metal real good. As if Lucky Frank wasn't already mad enough to spit nails. *Mofo.*

When I opened the door I stepped on two envelopes. Seemed like I was becoming the most popular slut in Pie Town. I sat down at the tiny kitchen table, threw back some tequila, and read the notes. The first one read: PACK YOUR BAGS. YOUR LEASE IS UP. The key and title to my old yellow Stude-baker were enclosed. The second note, which was folded into an itty-bitty square and took me for-fucking-ever to open, read: *I need to talk to you. I'm scared. Meet me tonight. Same place.* Looked like my little white rabbit'd had a change of heart. I took a couple of slugs of tequila and lit a smoke.

I was feeling real sick. Not just hangover sick, not just wanting-Creed sick; once-a-month female-sick. My ovaries were tender, a sweet dull ache in my belly. I wanted Daddy to rub it. *Oh, Daddy, where are you?* And then, right then, *kowabunga – kowabunga*: nine letters; bad – a heavy stream of bright red blood started to run down my legs, puddling up on the cheap speckled linoleum. *Speckled linoleum*: ten letters, two sets of five; very, very, good. I bent down and dipped my fingertips into the blood. *Blood*: five letters; good. Then I pressed my bloody fingertips against the dirty yellow wallpaper. I stood back and looked at the ten perfect fingerprints – made in blood. *Made in blood*: eleven letters; bad letters, very bad letters.

I caught my reflection in the mirror. *Big, big mistake.* I came to Pie Town looking for normalcy, anonymity – maybe a little refuge from the pain that just wouldn't let me be. I came looking to maybe quiet the voice that kept telling me I was worthless. But somehow, I'd ended up on a fast train to Weirdsville. And, as a sad matter of fact, it looked like I was about as far from normal as a gal could get before crossing the line of no return. But I was wrong. I'd already crossed that line. Thing was, I just didn't know it.

I waited till hell froze over, but Rabbit never showed. I needed smokes and booze – maybe a pack of Sno Balls. It was late. I'd have to hurry if I wanted to get to Anita's before closing. I took a shortcut through the back parking lot of Main Street Church. There was only one car in the lot, parked under the shadow of an overhang. It was dark-colored. It looked familiar. *Could it be?* My heart skipped a beat. *Daddy!* I rushed forward arsy-varsy. *Oh, Daddy!* It sure did look like … but … no, it wasn't. No orange pinstripes, no pinstripes, period. My heart sank. My stomach knotted. I passed the car and dreamily ran my hand along the side. *Oh, Daddy, where are you?* Suddenly I felt something sticky. I looked at my hand. I smelled it. Then I bent down and examined the spot where I had touched the metal.

The something on my hand was black; it smelled like paint. And there, hiding beneath the recently applied black paint, was a bright orange pinstripe. *What the fuck?*

■ ■ ■

Anita was out of Sno Balls. Anita was out of Ring Dings. I got the third best thing. Surprisingly, Devil Dogs, rot-gut, and cigarettes make for a decent snack.

I stared at Rabbit's note, trying to think clearly. *Javelin. Pinstripes. Postmarks. Daddy. Skinner. Spray paint. Rabbit. Alice. Maggie. Tommy. Lucky Frank. U.S. Marshal Dunk Hayward. Buddy Pinchback. Honey McGuinness. No job. No home. Attempted murder. Prison time.* Nothing made sense. Nothing made sense, cuz these were all just meaningless words now. Meaningless words with letters – letters that had to be counted! – letters that had to add up to five or multiples of five.

By the time I finished half the forty-rod and my second pack of Newports, I knew what was throwing me off track: five was an *uneven* number. *Even* numbers, *four-* letter words, or multiples of four . . . *that was my ticket back*. The problem was simple: how to get from odd to even.

I finished the fifth of whiskey and weighed the consequences of my solution. I read somewhere that the right half of the brain – the side that controlled the left hand – was mute. I opened my left palm and stared. Being that it was controlled by speechless matter, well, I figured maybe there wouldn't be such a fuss over the mess. I studied each finger. I gave the thumb and pinky a quick eighty-six. That narrowed it down to the index, middle, and ring. Being that I wasn't exactly what you'd call marriage material or the kinda gal a fella would bring home to Mom, and therefore being that I'd never be someone's wife, have a family, or live behind a white picket fence, well . . . *easy come, easy go.*

The first hack didn't go all the way through. The knife was big, but rusty. I gave it a couple more whacks and huzzah-huzzah-huzzah if the little sucker didn't go flying across the room and carom right into the middle of the bloody fingerprints on the wall, then drop to the floor with a little thump. I looked at my hand and smiled. There it was . . . an even four! *Pure fucking genius.*

I laid my head down on the table and closed my eyes. In my dream there was talk of me getting "orograted." And, by the end of the dream, I got orograted. Someone asked me if it was "some kinda pain," but before I could answer, I woke up . . . in some kinda pain.

Red was everywhere. Hands, arms, legs, hair, clothes, table, floor – covered in blood. I looked at my stub – a geyser of hot red and white corpuscles. I felt confounded, dizzy, and short of breath. *Think. Think. Stop the bleeding. Stop the pain.* I tried to stand but slipped and fell in the slithery gore. I used my right hand to sideslip across the floor to the kitchen closet. *Dish rag. Wrap stump in dish rag.* I reached the closet and knocked Lucky Frank's Winchester outta the way. *When had I propped it up against the door? Why was my blood oozing out from under the bottom of the closet door?*

I gripped the lever and struggled to pull myself up. But before I could, the closet door swung open.

■ ■ ■

The last thing I saw was Rabbit Rawlings, propped upright in my kitchen closet with a bullet hole through his forehead. The last thing I felt was the crushing weight of the albino's body as it fell forward and landed on top of me with a thud. And the last thought in my brain was: *Silly Rabbit, Trix are for kids.*

Bright-white snowflakes, jet-black squiggles, fluttering shapes of fluorescent orange and electric blue vibrating behind lighttight lids. Earsplitting high-pitched ringing and deafening subcutaneous rumblings inside a catatonic cranium. Rocketing bolts of unholy pain. *Welcome to Pay-the-Piper Time.*

"You have the right to remain silent. Anything you say or do can and will be used against you in a court of law."

My eyes opened. The badge said Springerville Detective Squad.

"You have the right to an attorney. If you cannot afford an attorney, one will be appointed to you. Do you understand these rights as they have been read to you?"

I nodded instinctively and looked around. The other three hospital beds were empty, but the room was crowded: two gumshoes, a couple of Jakes, Dunk Hayward, and a nurse who looked tougher than all the fellas put together. The room was yellow-green. The wall-mounted TV was off and pushed to the side. There was beeping apparatus, and a tube down my throat. Two IVs were taped to my right arm – one in the back of my hand, and one at the inner elbow. The tubes ran to two drip-bottles on a stand. I was wearing a festive floral Johnny shirt.

"I'm in a hospital," I said in a garbled voice.

My throat stung awful. I tried to yank the tube out, but couldn't – probably something to do with the fact that my right wrist was shackled to the bed rail. When I tried to move my left arm – which was bandaged to just below my armpit – I got a pain so bad I yelped.

The nurse pushed through the fellas. She took my temperature with an electronic thingy and wrote something on her clipboard. Then she took my blood pressure and pulse.

"Am I going to die?" I asked, with painful effort.

She ignored my question and turned towards The Law.

"That's all," she barked. "The patient has lost a lot of blood. She's scheduled for a second transfusion this afternoon. She's got systemic sepsis. We're pumping her full of antibiotics, but she's running a high fever. She's in pain, and she needs rest." She pointed towards the door. "Out."

She turned her back on them. The testosterone detail slowly formed a huddle in the middle of the room. The nurse picked a comb up from the bed table. Using the sharp pointy end, she tried to part my knotted hair, saying something about how ladies need to look good on the outside even when they don't feel good on the inside, but I squealed miserably. She inhaled deeply, made an exasperated huffing sound on the exhale, and swung around.

"Out, now!" she threatened, pointing the sharp end of the comb towards the group.

The cluster grudgingly started towards the door, quiet except for the Springerville detective who had read me my rights. He grumbled as he put his badge away, and held the door open while the others passed through. Then he turned and gave me the dead-eye.

"Officer Sanchez here will be sitting outside the room, in case you get any ideas about leaving." Officer Sanchez leaned into the room and nodded. Then the detective smiled and said, "Oh, I forgot to mention something. Honey McGuinness, you are under arrest for the murder of Rabbit Rawlings."

The door closed behind him. The nurse set the comb down and said, "Well, that's comforting." Then she loaded a large syringe and injected it into one of the IVs. The effect was immediate. *Oh, sweet Miss Emma.*

Before I slipped into a morphine stupor I had one thought: *What kinda low-down no-good jokers would saddle their kid with the name Rabbit?* And then another: *It's a cruel, cruel world.*

I got the "chuck" part of a chuckle out before everything went back to black.

"Inhale," a woman softly cooed in my ear.

It had no odor. It was thicker than water, slightly gooey, and trickling down from a wet cloth that was being held tightly over my nose and mouth. I touched my tongue to my lip; some slight taste of something . . . something, I don't know . . . *toxic*. I inhaled. Every cell in my body started to quiver pleasurably. I felt positively . . . *flammable*. *This* was some potent shit: eye-popping potent. My eyes popped open.

The cooing woman was standing over me. She wasn't actually a woman. She didn't look old enough to ride Barnstormer at Goofy's Wiseacre Farm without her mommy. She had a sweet smile, though. And if I had to be asphyxiated by someone, I was glad it was her.

"Shhhhhh," she cooed.

I blinked.

"Hello, Honey," a familiar male voice said, sounding cool as the other side of the pillow.

I blinked again and turned my head.

"*Creed?*" I bayed painfully against the crushing weight of the wet rag pressed against my mouth.

"More, Melody. She needs more," Creed whispered, with a devilish grin.

Melody removed one hand. I gasped for air. Melody dipped the cloth into a bowl of yellowish liquid.

"*That . . . embalming . . . fluid?*" I asked, in a breathy, painful, and semi-intelligible voice.

Melody giggled. Others giggled. Creed smiled and put his finger to his lips.

"Don't talk," he said in a soft, calm voice. "It's toluene. A very *special* potion. One hundred times more potent than rhinoceros horn. It's going to take your pain away. It's going to make you feel very . . . *special.*"

There were more giggles.

"No need to hold it down so tightly," Creed whispered to Melody. "She'll be a good girl." He looked at me. "Won't she?" I nodded slightly. His eyes sparkled. "Now, don't make a sound, sweet Jezebel." His voice was certain and assuring. "I'm taking you out of here, to someplace safe – somewhere where no one can hurt you ever again."

Melody laid the cloth lightly over my nose and mouth.

"You just breathe," she cooed into my ear. "We'll do the rest."

I breathed deeply, and with each breath I felt less pain and more . . . *special* . . . as in, hot and bothered and, apparently, a hundred times more sexually aroused than if I'd ingested rhinoceros horn.

Five or six people worked quickly, silently, while Creed directed traffic. They pulled plugs, disconnected tubes, removed tape. They pulled the needles out of my arm and extracted the tube from my throat. I smiled beneath the saturated cloth; I was feeling no pain. And, with each inhale, my smile grew broader. Everyone looked good enough to fuck. *Oh, toluene, where have you been all my life?*

They used a key to unlock the handcuffs. And by the time I was up and dressed in a pretty pink long skirt and white blouse, and headed out the hospital room door, I was mercifully lost in a warm, fuzzy, undulating cocoon of fleshy desire. Even Officer Sanchez – who was slumped against the wall in the corner with the tooth end of a familiar-looking comb sticking out of his bloody chest – looked like a wet dream.

"'It's a beautiful day in the neighborhood,'" I sang easily, finally free of the painful tube snaking down my throat. I recognized my voice. It was gravelly, full of bullpiss – the same bogus peace-and-free-love voice I shagged during my China-white years.

Creed pulled one of the beefcakes aside.

"Pinchback," he whispered in his ear. "Room three-oh-one." He nodded with his chin down the hall. "Meet you at the car."

■ ■ ■

The road went from straight, paved, and smooth to winding, dirt, and bumpy. I nodded out in the backseat, sandwiched between Creed on my right and two hunky young fellas on my left. Three gals, including Melody, and one fella, the driver, were packed into the front seat. From behind they looked equally appealing.

My head lolled about, eventually landing like a ton of bricks on Daddy's shoulder. Other than a few niggling distant thoughts – *I'm gonna be on* America's Most Wanted; *I'm gonna fry in the electric chair* – and a few discomfiting questions – *What the fuck is going on? How am I gonna get outta this jam?* – and a few disagreeable images of dead men looping around in my head – *Poor Rabbit; poor Officer Sanchez* – I was about as happy as a clam in high water and hotter than a six-peckered tom cat. And when I started to feel troubled or pained, well, I just sniffed more "Special-T" – code for the yellow liquid sex drug – from a dampened rag that was being passed around the car, and just like that, *Ba da, ba da, ba da, ba da . . . feelin' groovy.*

It was a long ride. I stared out the window, a mindless, wankered, happy smile plastered across my face, as the landscape changed from aureolin to tangerine to cobalt blue. By sundown it was an enchanting starry half-moon night.

"How're you feeling, baby?" Creed asked.

"User friendly," I giggled, which prompted chuckles all around.

We drove on, the only sound the rhythmic whir of the engine. We passed two large radio telescopes; backlit against the sky they looked like big black prehistoric monsters frozen in time. We passed a large stretch of high desert mesa with a lightning cloud hovering above it. Bolts of lightning streaked down from the cloud, striking giant poles that were evenly-spaced across the field. Large flashes of electricity sparked the sky, followed by the boom of rolling thunder. *This must be the place*, I thought. *The "lightning place" I've seen off in the distance nearly every day since I arrived in Pie Town.*

"The Lightning Field," Creed gently explained, reading my mind.

"Umm," I said, dreamily.

"In Quemado."

"Quemado," I repeated, dreamily.

"Man-made. 1977. Sculptor named De Maria. They call it "Land Art." *Land Art. Isn't that special.*

We drove down into a valley, crossed an arroyo, and started up into a mountain range.

"We're almost home, baby," Creed whispered.

I sat up tall. In the distance I saw clusters of light spread across a large expanse.

"Yellow trailer," I said, absently.

"Yellow trailer?" Creed snickered. "No!" he barked suddenly. "No more yellow trailer! That's over!"

He was right. That *was* over. And so was Alice and Romeo and my job and my famous high-priced cocktail, The Pie Slicer. And so was my life. Suddenly I felt like a big fat loser.

"Don't be an ungrateful girl," Creed warned, then softened and kissed my head. "Remember, home is where you love, not where you live."

Home is where you love, not where you live. There it was again. I could hear him now, Skinner P. Ochs: "Like my pa always said . . ." But that was once upon a time, and that time was over too.

I took several big whiffs of Special-T and the warm sexy feeling of pleasure returned. *Bye-bye, Loser; Hello, Hot Lips.* I smiled and sighed contentedly.

We approached the complex head-on, and stopped at the entrance. Two columns of light beamed down on us from spotlights affixed to either side of a large sign that arced high above a double-swing security gate. The sign was heavy-looking – iron, maybe. The design reminded me of the entrance to the Nazi concentration camps: *Arbeit macht frei,* "Work will make you free." *Very reassuring.* I took another big dose of Special-T.

An armed guard approached, cupped his hands, and pressed against the rear passenger window. Creed nodded, and the guard pressed a button. The gates swung in. As we drove through, I rubbernecked madly, but it was too dark to make out the inscription on the sign. Melody turned around and touched my knee tenderly.

"World Advocacy for Values in an Enlightened Society," she said proudly.

"You're one spicy meatball," I said, apropos of nothing but my hot box.

Creed snorted softly and Melody squeezed my hand understandingly.

"It's an academy of higher education," the hunky fella to my left explained.

"Ever eaten chicken snatchitori?" I asked him, half jokingly.

Soft titters trickled through the car.

"Enough about business," Creed scolded. "Now get over here. You're too far away."

He pulled me closer. Then he held the Special-T rag over my nose and mouth, put his free hand up my skirt, and started to massage my hoo-ha.

"*Oh, Professor*," I moaned.

He grinned glibly.

"I've got a very special *assignment* for you," he whispered.

He unzipped his fly; he wasn't wearing undies. *Hubba hubba.* I took hold of his hard longfellow.

"Time to cleanse the leper!" he howled, and pushed my head down. "Suck."

Well, he didn't have to tell me twice. I wanted to suck. I wanted to cleanse the leper. I loved the leper. *The more lepers the better!*

"That's what you wanted, isn't it? *Oooo, baby.* Your mouth was made to suck a big hard prick. Suck me good, baby."

I sucked him good, like a Eureka Mighty Mite. I couldn't get enough. Daddy was right again. My mouth *was* made to suck a big hard prick.

"Ooo, ooo, baby. Get ready for it. Here it comes. Open wide, good girl. That's right. *Here comes your medicine. Come on. Suck! Suck! Suck!*"

And just like that, before we rounded the third sharp curve in the winding dirt road, *kowabunga*, a mouth full of cum. *Mmm, mmm, good.*

I sat up, swallowed my medicine, and licked my lips. Daddy growled and went back to rubbing my muffin, and I started to writhe and wiggle against his hand. He leaned forward slightly and looked at the dreamboat to my left.

"Woman is a temptress, is she not? You hard? Show me."

Well, he didn't have to tell him twice. The hunkorama whipped out his stiff bugfucker. I took a big inhale of Special-T and smiled naughtily. Creed took my hand and wrapped it around the throbbing flesh.

"Honey, say hello to Hurricane."

I said hello to Hurricane, and Daddy said hello to my woogit, and there was some girl-on-girl action in the front seat, and Melody's head disappeared into the driver's lap, and the stud next to Hurricane started to play solitaire, and we continued to slowly wind our way up the road, and, well, it just felt right. Like everything was right in the world. Like blowing the old fella on my right and jacking off the young fella on my left in the backseat of a mobile orgy of quivering engorged genitalia and hot-blooded hootchy-kootch was about as routine as the seventh-inning stretch. And I thought: *Fuck Pie Town! Now* this *is the kinda normal a gal could get used to!*

We undulated our way past several well-lit outbuildings with folks moving about here and there, and Creed muttered words like "apprentice," "amplitude," "classroom," and "dorm." And as we rounded the final curve the fuckfest reached an enthusiastic collective climax in near-perfect synchronicity. Hurricane jizzed in my hand and thanked me. *How cute is that?*

We pulled up in front of a large rectangular single-story ranch house with a low-pitched gable roof, deep-set eaves, and shuttered windows. It was built of brick and wood. Smoke was coming from a stack.

"Home sweet home," Creed whispered in my ear.

After a few moments of clothes straightening and a round of polite "Thank-yous" that were so right and proper you'd've thought we'd just had tea and crumpets instead of a team cream, the group piled out. Creed reached in and picked me up in his arms. I held the Special-T rag over my nose and inhaled the pain-relieving aphrodisiac.

"I'm going to teach you what it means to be a real woman. I'm going to excise your false idols; liberate you from cognitive guilt, shame, self-loathing; alter your physiognomy. I'm going to pry that nail from your wing and teach you how to fly. What do you have to say about that?"

"Rots of ruck," I giggled.

He laughed – a deep, endless belly laugh that echoed through the still night.

"You're a real find, Honey McGuinness. A real find."

He carried me across the threshold like I was a blushing bride.

"Welcome to the Land of Milk and Honey!"

"There are no accidents in life. Everything has already been written. You, me, everything. You don't know it, because there are monsters in your dreams. But I know it. I was chosen. I am *The Gift*. I am *your* gift. I am *The New Light*. I am here to right the wrong. I am *The Force of Nature*, the *Infinite Force*. I am God. I am man. Through me you are born. Through me you are consecrated. I am *The Beast*. You are my attendant. I am *Pure Flesh*, accountable only to the laws of nature. No man can contain me. I am above the law. And through me you are now above the law. The unbelievers can't touch you anymore! You're protected by The New Light. You're mine. You belong to me. I chose you. The believers told me you were trouble. They said I needed to get rid of you. So I tested you. But you didn't run away. You stayed. So I came for you. And I *saw* you. I *saw* what they could *never* see. And the unbelievers, the outsiders, they will *never* find you now. If they come looking, I am ready. *The Prophet of Doom awaits all contenders of Creed Kurgan!* They are doomed – all of them, because they have lost their way. They have corrupted the natural order with their perversion. They have ceded manhood, traded the blade for the chalice! They are cunt-struck lumps of flaccid flesh, led by an impotent petticoat government. No! Don't worry about them, good girl! You are safe now! You have a home! No one will hurt you! You are with the Prophet now! You are with the *amplitude* of the Prophet! My warriors will lay down their lives for you. You are the *primal typos* – the female archetype – the original form of which all else is a copy! You are the divine mind – the collective unconscious! You are on a new path to salvation! You are The Mother of the Fourth Wave!"

Holy fucking frijole.

He slipped his hand under the blanket and stuck one finger up my bazoo and one up my quivering yum-yum. Then he gave me a cheery Prophet of Doom grin.

When hard luck falls, it just keeps on falling. The thought might've sent a gal who was on the lam from the law for first degree murder – who was so hurtin' for it that she got cock-smitten with a greasy ole mac daddy horn-dog cuntophile who, funnily enough, also turned out to be the jacked-up New Light Prophet-of-fucking-Doom for some almost certainly murderous wannabe-Charlie-Manson sex cult, and a gal who was otherwise friendless, penniless, and homeless – into a steep vertical speed wobble . . . but not this gal. Cuz, in actual fact, I was in an erotomaniacal dope-addled stupor – fed by a mainline IV of self-administered sweet Miss Emma and a steady inhalation of Special-T pumped into my nose through a nasal tube – and couldn't hardly tell La-La-Land from reality.

"In the land of the blind," the Prophet of Doom continued, "the one-eyed man is king."

I hit the red button on the doohickey in my right hand with my thumb in rapid-fire succession so Miss Emma could hold back the unpleasantly encroaching reality. She did her job.

"Ain't it the truth," I mumbled.

The truth? The truth was that I'd been secreted away and hopped-up near comatose in blissful bamboozlement for days, maybe weeks – with a head full of unasked questions. *Was the room really filled with burning incense and candles? Were serene young gals dressed in pink and skin-headed young fellas dressed in blue caressing my body, whispering sweet nothings, tweaking my nipples, singing me lullabies, giving me sponge baths, changing my bed pan? Were there daily bedside vigils praying that I'd pull through? Did a doctor say it was "touch and go?" Did he say I was "fevered and delirious?" Did someone call the doctor Joe Cocker? Did someone remove the bandage on my left hand? Did Creed suck my stump? Was there a thump-thump-thump thundering under my bed? Was it so strong that each time it thumped the bed jigged? Who told Creed that I was "trouble"? Who said he had to "get rid" of me?* And then there were those other pesky little questions: *Who killed Rabbit Rawlings? Who killed Officer Sanchez? Was Buddy Pinchback pushing up daisies? Was I responsible for their murders? What did it all mean? Was I dreaming? Was I just stuck in some gruesome nightmare?*

It was a strain to think. But confused, strung out mute, and hopeless as a penny waiting for change, I still knew the score: Creed Kurgan was right; I was out of options. Under the circumstances, Daddy *was* king.

The king? He came every day. And he didn't just feed the kitty. Oh, no. Daddy was amped. He did the Bombay-roll, pissed-in-the-dugout, ploughed-the-back-forty, and moved up and down Route Sixty-Nine. He scarfed furburgers and ate the last donut in the shop, then came back for more. And amid multiple drug-enhanced super-fly bump-and-grinds, shake-and-shivers, and explosive splatters of goose grease and splooge, Creed talked . . . and talked . . . and talked. And if anything other than a moan or whimper started outta my mouth, he put his finger to his lips and told me, "Shhh."

"Save your strength. Lay back. Close your eyes. Listen. Breathe. Take. Receive."

"Doc says you're nearly out of the woods. The infection's under control. Fever's gone, three days now. Your finger is healing." He took hold of my left hand and examined my stub, smiled and whispered, "You are a real find. Yes, you are." He sucked the stump then gently laid my hand back down on the blanket.

"Another few days, you'll be out of bed. But be forewarned. You've got twenty-five years of iniquity to cleanse. You've already started to purge – the fever, the blood loss – but it's not over. It's only the beginning. The poison will continue to leach from your pores, your bowels, every orifice. And the purer you become, the more the *evil* will cling to your flesh. But don't worry! I am your savior! I will protect you! God's *amplitude* will protect you! You will not suffer through purification! No! You will *never* suffer again! Remember, sweet Jezebel, *you have already endured!*" He leaned over and licked the sweat off my forehead. "You have lived outside the movement. You have lived in a purposeless society built on lies, *and you have survived!* And soon you will be ready to know the Truth! To follow the New Path! You will be *un*-corrupted! You will be my Vestal Virgin! You will learn the Book of Rules! You will be the Mother of all mothers! You cannot yet see because you have been blinded and corrupted! But I am your eyes now! See through my eyes! Rely on me! You are my vessel! I will fill you! I will protect you from those who will contend! You will be my wife! I will love . . ."

I closed my eyes and clicked the red button again and again: I couldn't get Miss Emma into my veins fast enough. Creed continued to talk. I didn't have to listen; I'd heard all his insane hooey before. But somehow, little by little, well . . .

Maybe it was just that *when you ain't got nothin', you got nothin' to lose.* Or maybe it was just the exotic pizzazz of palliative and titillative dope, or my greedy, swollen love-button and gluttonous, inflamed hoo-hoo that weren't about to rat out the only fella who'd ever rocked their worlds – no matter how much arkymalarky came outta his mouth – or maybe it was just the constant adoring TLC by Creed and his "amplitude." Whatever the maybe, I was still a narcissistic Angel of Death, a gutless spawn whose broken promise sent her mother to a lonely plunging death, the punk pubescent who'd held the cold muzzle of a Raven to the forehead of her own flesh and blood and pulled the trigger without a second thought, the sadomasochistic cocksmith who only stopped playing the love-equals-death game because zipping up body bags became a predictable bore. I was the pathetic excuse of a soul who ached for another woman's man, the sniveling gimp who silently skulked off into the sunset cuz she couldn't stand the sight of her own sorry reflection in the eyes of that other woman's man, the pitiful self-centered junkie who let down a bighearted wide-assed pal named Alice and her mutt Romeo. So why would a gal like me mean anything to anyone? She wouldn't; she never did. But then . . . there they were, 24/7: Daddy and his amplitude – showing me the love, treating me like I meant something to someone.

So's I started to think, *OK, so maybe I'll never be number eighty-seven on the "Welcome to Pie Town" sign, but that doesn't mean I can't be numero uno at the World Advocacy for Values in an Enlightened Society! OK, so maybe I'll never be June Cleaver or birth the Beav, but that doesn't mean I can't be Mrs. Spanked-and-Tanked Prophet of Doom, mother of The Fourth fucking Wave!* Hey, when life hands you lemons . . .

So, well, little by little, cult-leader Kurgan started to seem less like a demented homicidal fuck-freak, and more like . . . my only way out. And, then, *kowabunga*, it happened – a funny little question took hold of my drug-dependent addlebrain, and I couldn't shake it loose: *What the hell, why not just drink the Kool-Aid?*

■ ■ ■

"Don't be rude," Creed scolded.

We weren't alone. A tattooed bull-dyke in tight leather pants and a wife-beater was standing next to Creed. *Tiny titties for such a big gal.*

"Say hello to Big Tiny."

"Hardy har," I giggled.

Big Tiny giggled a tiny giggle that softened her face and caused crinkles around her eyes.

"Big Tiny's an artist in body modification. Her work pushes the bounds of dimensional reality. She plays with light and shadow, complexity and simplicity."

He turned his head and nodded with his chin. I followed his lead to a nearby table covered in blue plastic. In addition to bottles and bandages of varying sizes, there were several instruments – meticulously lain out – that looked like maybe they'd been borrowed from the local torture chamber. *At's a no good.* I bit my lower lip, hit the red button, and inhaled.

"Body modification," I echoed, sounding like a zonked-out parrot.

"It's nothin' bad," Big Tiny said in a comforting, high, tiny voice. "I do Tebori – an ancient Japanese method of tattooing."

"Hand-poked," the Prophet of Doom explained.

"*Oooooocccch,*" I slurred.

Big Tiny tilted her head sympathetically. I tried to muster a smile.

"Big Tiny is my gift to you! A pre-wedding gift!" Creed said, his eyes wild with excitement. "The first of many!"

He cranked up the demand valve on the tank and a blast of Special-T filled my nostrils, making me feel warmer and fuzzier all over. He threw the blankets off of me. Then the two of them took a step closer and studied my naked body. Big Tiny ran her hand across my belly. She had a light touch. *Gimme more.* I wiggled and moaned. Creed grinned approvingly.

"She'll have to be shaved," Big Tiny whispered.

"All in a day's work," Creed said, with a wide grin. Big Tiny giggled. "Have a seat in the living room," he said to her. "I'll let you know when she's ready."

After Big Tiny left the room, I said, "But, Daddy, I —"

"Shhh. No questions. Trust me."

He gave me a quick, cold stare. I licked my lips.

"Spread your legs."

He took a dildo from the drawer next to the bed and covered it with lube.

"Hold this."

He went to the end of the bed and sat down. He pulled me towards him, keeping my legs open. He licked my girlfriend then fucked me lightly with his tongue. I panted and pressed against his mouth.

"Hold off," he laughed.

He got up and returned with a bowl of warm water and a razor.

"Give it to me," he ordered.

I handed him the slippery dildo. He circled it around the lips of my conchita, then pushed it in and out, in and out. I squirmed and whimpered for more.

"Hold still."

He shoved the dildo all the way into me.

"Close your legs a little."

He rubbed warm soapy water over my pubes and started to shave me, every once in a while stopping to fuck me with the dildo. He was slow and careful. When he nicked me he was quick to lick the wound. When he'd finished the job he brought me a mirror.

"Like a virgin!" he said, breathing hard. "Soon the transformation will be complete! Just like I said!"

He unzipped his pants. Hard, as usual. He pulled the dildo out and dropped it to the floor. Then he held my legs up in the air, spread wide. He fucked me, growling as he watched his willy move in and out of my snatch.

"Oh, I like what I see, baby. Oh, yeah. You like it? You want it? Oh, yeah. Get ready for it, baby."

"Ready . . . ready," I gasped.

"Good," he groaned and pumped my hole like a piston. "I'm ready! You ready?"

I was ready. But suddenly he slammed on the brakes.

"Stop! No! You shouldn't do this!" he bellowed. "She is Creed Kurgan's virgin! You have to wait! Wait until you are united!"

He looked at me, through me, his eyes glazed. I didn't know who he was talking to or what had possessed him, but my undulating body was on the verge of another miraculous O, and if I had any say-so in the matter he was gonna finish what he started.

"No. No. It's OK," I said breathlessly. "I need . . . I need my *medicine*. Please. C'mon. Give it to me, Daddy."

"No. Daddy has to wait!"

"No. No," I panted. "Tell Daddy it's OK. Just this once."

Creed looked down at my body, then pulled my legs so wide apart that I thought I might split like a wishbone.

"Well, maybe just this once," he beamed. He started to pump into me again – moving his shaft in and out of my dripping pussy – deep and hard, shallow and gentle. When I started to screech like a macaca he pulled his prick out and polished me off with his fingers. He laughed and snarled and jerked off onto my belly. He took my finger and stuck it into the wad of warm sticky jizzum, then stuck it in his mouth and sucked it off. He did the same thing, but this time stuck the cum-loaded digit into my mouth. He massaged the remaining gob over my breasts and nipples and kissed me hard. Then he went to the door.

"She's ready."

The air was thick with the smell of sex. Big Tiny stared at my belly. She seemed kinda tense.

"Loosen up," Creed said, slapping Big Tiny on the back.

She looked at me. "Are you sure—"

"Don't talk to her!" he snapped. "Talk to me!"

"Is she—"

"Are you deaf? I told you! She's ready."

Big Tiny gave him the thumbs-up and walked towards the table. Creed took a large loaded syringe and injected the contents into my IV.

"You won't feel any pain," he whispered and kissed my forehead.

The room became intensely colored – bright, primary, liquid colors. Big Tiny loomed over me. She looked cartoonish, glossy, supersized, almost comical. I stared at her arms, mesmerized by a particular tattoo that ran from her wrist to her shoulder. As she moved her arm, the ink started to peel away from her flesh and float in the air, in a line – a black broken line – a black, broken, wavy line. *Black broken wavy line?* I'd seen it before. *Where? When?* A stab of pain interrupted my thoughts. I opened my mouth to protest the "hand-poking" into my belly with a sharp bamboo needle, but instead of yelping, I laughed. Big Tiny and Creed looked at me, their faces exaggerated, contorted, clownish. Creed said something, his words slow, incomprehensible. Big Tiny went back to poking deeper and deeper into my flesh. I could hear the crackling sound of the weight of my body and the drip drip drip of blood on the plastic tarp beneath me. The rank stench of sex and blood filled my lungs. I turned and stared out the large picture window and watched the flashes of light coming from the distant lightning fields of Quemado. Then I heard Daddy tell me to hold still. And when I didn't, I heard him call out, and next thing I knew Creed was holding my legs, and Hurricane was holding my right arm, and another fella was holding my left. And I looked back and forth between them a couple of times and, well, either Hurricane had an identical twin brother, or I was seeing double.

■ ■ ■

Five words carved into my belly, hand poked by Big Tiny in the ancient Japanese method. It looked pretty enough, though a little scabbed over. A snake-shaped arrow ran down and pointed at my bald little kitty. The words read: THIS PUSSY BELONGS TO CREED. It was official.

"Rise from the ashes!"

I was nauseous, dizzy, confused, trembling. My head hurt so bad it itched. My nose was running, my body aching, my heart pounding. I had goose bumps, cold flashes, hot flashes, and a shrill ringing in my ears.

"You are the Phoenix!"

"Not unless the Phoenix feels like shit warmed over."

"You are the immortal bird!"

"What's that constant fucking pounding? Make it stop," I rubbed my temples.

"You have died, burst into flames, and now you are reborn from your own ashes!"

Creed threw back the blankets. I pulled them up.

"I'm cold. I don't feel good. I wanna go back to sleep."

He pulled the blankets off again.

"No! No more sleep, sweet Jezebel. You've been asleep your entire life! It's time to wake up! Make up for lost time!"

The last thing I wanted to be was conscious. *Give me drugs.* I pulled the blankets back over me and clicked the red button. Bupkis. I inhaled. Bupkis. Creed held up the ends of the tubes, detached from the morphine drip and the Special-T tank. He gave me the Prophet of Doom smile and waggled them teasingly, cruelly. I grabbed for them. He knocked my hand away.

"Uh oh," I said. *I'm not drugged. I'm not under the influence. I'm sober. Fuck. Panic.* Sweat beaded up on my forehead and upper lip. "Drugs. I need drugs," I said, unnerved.

"She sweats," he said, coldly.

I looked at his face – like I was seeing it for the first time. It was hard, ugly. And it was there. I could see it. I could smell it: evil. Sweat started to run down my face.

"Oh, don't fret. I've got a very, very *special* treat in store for you. I would've introduced it into you sooner, but Doc Cocker doesn't like to take chances: 'The wrong combination of drugs can cause an overdose.' So I had to wait till the opiates and chemicals were out of your system. It's been a week." He held up the tube to the morphine drip and shrugged. "No more." Then he held up the Special-T tube and grinned. "We'll see how good of a girl you are."

My body started to convulse.

"I need Doc Cocker."

"You're all right. You've been through the worst of the withdrawals already."

"Why? Why are you doing this?" I said, my voice shaky.

"It's part of the *process*," he scolded, like I should've known what the fuck he was talking about.

"What *process*?"

"Poor thing." He shook his head and tsk-tsked the tragedy of my igno-rance. "The process of purification, of course! The process of excising shame! The process of re-formation from street whore to Vestal Virgin! The process of mutation from barrenness to incubator!" He threw his head back and bayed.

Excising? Reformation? Mutation? Sounded like I was in for a world of pain. And experience had taught me that there was no bargaining with the Devil. I had to get outta there bahli-bahli, but I was in an awful bad way. *Houston, we've got a problem. Think. Think. You've been in jams before. There must be a way out. You're a smart girl. Yes, I am!* The Raven. It had one bullet in the chamber. It was in a box, in Pie Town. If I could just get my heater . . .

"I need my stuff – personal stuff – from Pie Town."

"Don't you understand? You don't have "personal stuff" anymore! You don't even have a past anymore!"

"I want out!"

"No! No! No out! No leaving! No looking back!"

Think again, Honey. Think. My heart raced so's I thought it would burst open my chest. My stomach knotted tight like a fist. My eyelids twitched and my body shook. Thick strings of dangling snot mixed with salty sweat and ran into my mouth. I couldn't think beyond the misery.

"Drugs, please."

"Besides," he said, ignoring my plea, "if I let you leave you'll be arrested." He grinned sarcastically. "Seems you've been a very bad girl. Seems you've been killing people."

"I didn't kill anyone!"

"You're wanted for murder. Two counts in the first degree, one in the second."

Two counts? Three counts? My stomach sank.

"But I didn't kill anyone," I said in feeble protest.

"You're sexy, but not all that clever. Seems you didn't clean up your mess after killing poor Mr. Rawlings. They've got fingerprints, blood evidence—"

"I didn't—"

"Still," he interrupted, "for a prosecutor, relying solely on such evidence comes at a risk. The defense will play the tampering-with-evidence card. They'll call into question the chain of custody and so on. Seems jurors have a thing for believing the worst about our men in blue. And it only takes one juror – one reasonable doubt. In order to assure a guilty verdict – maybe even up the ante to a capital offense – they'd need, well, something more . . . convincing . . . irrefutable. The murder weapon, for instance. They say the caliber of the bullet in the boy's head was the same caliber as the ones used in your shooting spree in the bar in town – the same caliber used in a certain rifle stolen from the back of a certain pickup truck. You know, to really put the last nail in your coffin, they'd need that rifle, wouldn't they? But, the thing is, they can't find it."

"I didn't kill Rabbit! Why would I?"

"Ah, motive!" he said, shaking his head thoughtfully. "Well, it seems that young Mr. Rawlings was a very bad boy – vandalized the side of your trailer with some very ungentlemanly language. And, rumor has it that you were going to make sure he paid for it."

I was confused. The only person I'd told about the "Go home slut" message was . . .

"*Alice?* Alice *wouldn't* . . . I'm on her list. She's my friend."

"You don't have any friends," he grinned cruelly. "Except for the amplitude, and," he pointed to his chest with his thumb, "me, of course. I'm your best friend now. You belong to me. If you need a reminder, look."

He threw the blanket off, exposing my belly: THIS PUSSY BELONGS TO CREED. He ran his fingers over the tattoo. His touch gave me the heebie-jeebies. His face was crimson red, his eyes blazing. He smiled devil-ishly. The sadistic modicking manny-jammer was really getting his rocks off.

"No one's gonna believe I killed Rabbit cuz of some fucking graffiti," I said, trying to rally.

"Granted, by itself, it seems like a pretty flimsy motive. But it would become much less flimsy if they had something . . . more convincing . . . irrefutable. A videotape showing you repeatedly bashing the poor boy's head against a brick wall, for instance."

Fuck. Fuck. Fuck.

"Drugs, please. I need drugs. Please."

"Now," he continued indifferently, "as long as you stay here with me there won't be any problems. The rifle and videotape are securely hidden. As long as you are a good girl, they'll stay that way. And, when you become Mrs. Creed Kurgan, those two items will disappear forever. On the other hand, if you should leave . . . " He turned his palms up and made a face, like the matter would be out of his hands.

I rubbed my temples. He had me by the short and curlies.

"Officer Sanchez is another story. Seems in that case, they actually have the murder weapon, a comb with a particularly sharp end, with your finger-prints on it. And Buddy Pinchback, well, it seems somebody didn't want him to be around to press charges – so that somebody pulled the plug on the poor man while he lay in a coma – a coma caused, it seems, in a certain shooting spree at a bar. The cops figure Honey McGuinness killed Officer Sanchez and then decided – since he was just down the hall, and she might as well make sure none of her victims could talk – to get rid of Buddy, before making her escape."

"That's a joke! I was handcuffed. I couldn't even—"

"Yes! You may have had help! They were hoping that recorded video from inside the hospital would have revealed the events – identified any person or persons who may have aided and abetted in your crimes. Unfortunately, the critical security cameras had been blacked out with spray paint. However, the officials did get one very promising lead."

His eyes pierced into me like daggers.

"Stop," I moaned, and closed my eyes. I couldn't take anymore.

"Seems the cowboy you stole that rifle from wasn't feeling too kindly towards you. Seems he likes to walk the interstate late at night – when he can't sleep. Seems he saw you on that same interstate." He raised his eyebrows, suggestively.

"So, I fucked him—"

"No! No! Not that time!" he bellowed. "Thanks to your Redeemer, those whorish activities will soon be forgiven! No, it was another time: the time you made a call . . . from the payphone."

He watched me intently as the news sank in. Goosebumps covered my body and I shivered. Tears joined the mix of bodily fluids streaming down my face. He reached towards me. I batted his hand away. He grabbed and squeezed. The wound was healed, but the tip of my stump was hypersensitive. I yelped. He squeezed harder.

"So, being that detectives detect, well, they traced the call you made from that payphone. And they found out that it belonged to an out-of-town cop."

"Skinner Ochs," I whispered.

He studied my face intently, looking for a reaction. I tried not to give him one.

"You're hurting me! Let go!"

He scoffed and continued. "It seems that you and this . . . Skinner . . . were involved in some kind of trouble a while back – trouble that resulted in several dead bodies. So, they gave this Officer Ochs a call. And being that law enforcement types like to accommodate each other – you know, 'brothers in blue,' as they say – this Officer Ochs obliged the detectives by coming to Pie Town to talk things over. In fact, he made it a family affair. Seems they've been talking things over for . . ."

Skinner was in Pie Town? Skinner and Mary and Rosa and Ruthie were in Pie Town? A sharp pain shot up my arm.

"You're hurting me! Let go!"

He released my hand. I started to seize. He held me down firmly while the convulsion cycled intensely through my body.

"Relax, sweet Jezebel," he said gently. "Surrender." He wiped my forehead. "You know," he whispered, "sometimes it's just easier not to have a choice."

I wouldn't know the difference; I've never had one.

"Sometimes Daddy knows best."

Sometimes dead is better.

My body stilled.

"You need drugs."

Though the seizure had completely zapped my strength, I managed to agree.

He walked across the room and put on "London Calling" by The Clash, and cranked it up loud. He came back with a bag in one hand and a tiny canister and a balloon in the other. He set the bag down. Then he screwed something to the top of the canister and it made a hissing noise. Then he put the balloon over the top and it began to fill up.

"I knew the first time I saw you that you were the one. I've been looking for you for my whole life. I've had hundreds of women, maybe thousands. But it's always been you I was looking for. And now that I have you, I'm going to Deliver you! I'm going to make you a virgin. I'm going to make you my wife. I'm going to love you! And together we will bring about the Fourth Wave – the fourth and final coming!"

Whatever, crazy fucker. Just give me the drugs.

He pulled the inflated balloon off the canister and inhaled, then took in a gulp of air, then exhaled the combination back into the balloon. Then he inhaled and exhaled a couple of times.

"This your first whippit?" I nodded that it was and he explained, "Happy gas. It'll take the edge off."

He held the balloon to my lips, and I inhaled and exhaled several times. I got an immediate rush. My head filled with tiny tickling bubbles. I got the giggles. He took the balloon and tied the end. Then he opened the bag. He told me to "open up" and poured a very large mound of dried powdery substance into my mouth. Then he poured the remainder of the bag into his own.

"Psilocybin! Magic mushrooms! The holy sacrament of the Creed of Kurgan!"

The Creed of Kurgan looked completely mad: big, crazy eyes thickly glazed over; a frozen, demonic oversized smile; a deep, unearthly cackle.

Oh, God. Was his head gonna start spinning? Was he gonna say, "Keep away! This sow is mine"? Oh God. I was in way over my head. It was enough to make a gal start counting again. What was I gonna do? What could I do? Only one thing: think about it later.

I inhaled and exhaled into the balloon and waited for fungal atonement.

"Don't worry, good girl. It'll be over soon. It's all part of the process. It's all . . . "

His words were like pins – each one popping one of the funny tiny bubbles that were taking me away from the grim reality. *Either shut up, you jive-ass crackpot, or shoot me now and put me out of my misery. Or . . .*

This situation wasn't just some bad case of the simples. Till I could think on my feet, I needed total oblivion. I needed the full monty: sex, drugs, and rock'n'roll. *Two out of three just wasn't gonna cut it.*

"Fuck me."

His eyes flashed.

"Fuck me."

"Now, *that's* my girl!!" He pulled the blankets down, and tweaked my nipples hard. "Five minutes, your mouth will feel numb. Twenty minutes, you'll be flying so high you might never come down!"

He made a low, slow grunt, and worked his way down and into my poon.

"My sweet virgin," he whispered. "Close your eyes. Relax. Let go of your fears and negativity. We don't want you to have a bad trip, do we? No! So, let's think positively! Let's be grateful for all the good things in your life! There is *so much* for you to be grateful for! Think about it. You're safe. You're cared for. You're loved. You've got everything you need . . . everything you'll *ever* need. You are destined for greatness! All you have to do now is let the psychedelic sacrament transport you to new realms of consciousness. Let the shrooms open your mind, free you from gravity."

I closed my eyes, and he kissed each one lightly. He moved his finger expertly in and out of my hot, oozing box. Slowly my mouth went numb; my muscles went limp. Then the drug came on fast. I started to feel completely unruffled. I started to feel hot and light and fuzzy. I started to feel . . . like I was somewhere else; like I was someone else. *Bless you, Dr. Leary.*

Creed fucked me. His penis and my vagina: *How could any two things be so perfectly designed?* His penis – big, hard, penetrating. My vagina – soft, elastic, self-lubricating. Our ten thousand combined nerve-endings mingled in a wild orgy of perfectly indescribable pleasure.

"Yes, my sweet Jezebel," he said, filling my ever-expanding vessel in slow rhythmic motions – five shallow thrusts, one deep – "you are destined to awake! And when you do, you will no longer be the egalitarian goddess worshipped in prehistoric times! You will no longer be the great mother whose image is on display from the caves of Lascaux to the caves of the Balkans! You will no longer be the matriarch of the Paleolithic and Neolithic ages! No! When you awake, you will be the Great Mother of the Fourth Wave! You will be the embodiment of the Natural Order, the New Light, the New Path!! *You will trade your chalice for my blade!*"

He pumped harder. My swollen rosebud started to emit ecstatic quivering electrical signals, transmitting an urgent message to my hyper-alert receptors – flashing red lights: Warning! Warning! Code Red! *Tsunami just offshore!*

"Gimme your blade, Daddy!" I hollered, and watched each letter float out of my mouth and ascend into the air like a Technicolor ribbon.

"Oh, I'll give you my blade!" he howled. "And you will be healed! Tonight you will be healed! Tonight you will succumb!" He laughed maniacally and plunged deeper and faster. "Oh, yes! You are the Phoenix reborn from your own ashes!" He drooled. "You have died! You have been reborn! You are immortal!"

We were one thing, one rapturous, grinding, orgasmic organism of male and female perfection. We were indivisible – merged of heart and mind, soul and spirit, and smoldering insatiable genitalia.

The master clitoromaniac gave me the whole enchilada – his full bag of tricks – beginning with his thumb lightly vibrating around my love-bud in rapid circular motions. Then he began to drive into me and our bodies flailed violently like fish out of water, and just as we reached simultaneous climax we reached hysterical laughter and we each shouted out. He: *Make me a Daddy, Mother!* Me: *The Devil made me do it!* He: *You will birth a nation!* Me: *Yippee yi-o ki-a!* And while he continued to shout – and cuz I had a severe case of whiplash from the emotional extremes of the night's events – a thought started to creep up like a thief, a thought whose middle name was "bad-fucking-trip-guaranteed-or-money-back." I blocked it at the entrance to my mind and told it to am-scray, butt out, put a sock in it. It pressed against me and started to murmur. So, I made a deal: I'd give it a thought – one thought, one time, in a whisper – and then it had to go away, and stay away. It agreed.

"There's one secret that's worse than the worst secret kept by victims of sexual abuse, one thing worse than the unspeakable crimes themselves, one thing beyond the horror that breaks a soul and binds it up in unappeasable shame and guilt. Only one thing. One secret. And that secret is: Sometimes it feels good."

Kneeling bodies. Black silhouettes. Lizard-like flicking tongues feeding on magic mushrooms. Communion. Reunion. Holy Mother. Holy Father. The profession: confession. Supercharged substratum. Supersonic waves. Longitudinal liquid. Transverse plasma. Traversing matter. Spread-eagle on a cloud. The speed of sound. The sound of light. The color of music. The Amazing Lazy Susan! Interchanging organisms. Allocating orgasms. Gyrating flesh. Rising. Falling. Expanding. Contracting. The aspiration: penetration. The amplitude! The dissolution of the id! The ascent of the galactic wave! The super-excellence of the six-sided square!

■ ■ ■

"You know Hurricane, of course." "His brother, Jet." "Identical twins." "Jet with the forehead indent." Double-take. *The Guthrie twins?* "Goose." *Jackson?* "You know this girl." *Daisy?* "Daisy Clover." Hurricane, Jet, Goose, Rowdy, Snake, Will, Pug, Flash, Melody, Joy, Patience, Angel, Daisy . . . *Oh, where have the young girls gone? Gone to here . . . every one.*

"Come close, my amplitude! Gather around. Tonight *I* am your professor! Children, we are not about to enter a paradise like the ideal of law or otherworldliness or surrender or action or negation or harmony. No! We are on the precipice of the Fourth Wave! The Final Wave! Children, I have mandated cohabitation, but I have forbidden direct transfer of seminal fluid between vehicle and vessel. I have, myself, constrained my holy emissions to your non-procreating orifices. I have done this not to deny you, but to ensure prophetic succession! I have been looking . . . looking for the right receptacle! I have been looking for the right vessel to receive my sacred fluid! And I have found it! Now, come. Bow to your God, kiss your father's feet, and he will show you the womb through which will come the birth of our nation!

"Origins: The Female Archetype. The original form from which all else is copied. To Aquinas it has its location in the divine mind. To Jung it refers to the primordial forms of the collective unconscious. Look in front of you. Look with your eyes, your minds, your bodies! You are blessed to witness the *original form!*

"In the universal scheme of things we are tiny, insignificant, vulnerable creatures. We are sinners! We are corrupt, perverse! We are homosexuals! We are rapists and whores! But this! *This* is not insignificant! *This* is our future! Look! Look at nature in the process of purification! See the defiled flesh re-forming – becoming what it once was and will soon be again: pure! Look closely! For, unless we are in harmony with this infinite force of nature, we cannot hope to survive.

"Focus! Relax! Breathe! Turn up the music! Take the sacrament! Open up! Come! Come! Open up for us! Look children. The universe revealed! The vagina! The vulva! The sexual organs just beneath the fatty pad covering the pubic bone. Look how it fits perfectly into my hand. Look how I cup the entire universe! And look as I spread these lips. These lips! The labia majora! And look as I spread them further apart. Look how the labia majora enclose the smaller folds – the labia minora. These labia protect the entrance to immorality . . . and immortality!

"Look at the face of your mother now. What do you see? Her face is flushed, her ears are red, her breathing is rapid, her nipples are hard! Come, my children! Touch, feel how the fire of nature has been heightened by our exploration. Feel how your own nature has been heightened. Now open up! Free yourselves! Expose yourselves! Feel yourselves! Don't be ashamed! I am with you! I open myself up with you! Look! Your father is erect! Your mother is wet! Feed yourselves! Free yourselves! Don't be afraid!

"You, on your knees. Now, watch closely. This labia majora and minora not only protect the entrance to the cunt. These folds also shield the clitoris, a tiny organ richly supplied with blood vessels and nerves. Like the male penis, the clitoris swells with blood and becomes sensitive during sexual arousal. Watch as I massage it. Try it yourself. Good. Yes! That's right! Now you, on your knees! Grip the vulva, feel the perfection of the shape in the palm of your hand. Arouse the clitoris with your mouth. Lick it, suck it, play with it. Use your whole mouth. Taste the inside of the labia, search the tiny organ. That's good. Look how the cunt drips! Now it's your turn, Goose. Oh, look how hungry he is! Look how his prick grows! Look how he massages her clit. Oh, suck her good, boy! Push! Push your tongue deep inside. Once you pass the lips you will enter the vessel. The vessel is protected by one mucosal layer, one muscularis layer and then the vaginal wall. Under the mucosal layer is a layer of strong interwoven muscle fibers. The folds in the inner mucosal layer, called rugae, straighten out during intercourse, as the receptor expands to receive the swollen cock. Look how nature has swollen your father's prick! Look at the oozing cunt. Massage yourselves, boys and girls. Arouse your sleeping sex! Transform yourselves into juicy, dripping fuck holes and hard-gunner cunt hunters!

"Next. Come up. Use your fingers and your mouth to explore your mother's hole – feel it, taste it, smell it. Stick your finger inside the enigmatic entryway. How warm and soft and safe it feels! Stick your tongue inside, lick the ambrosia. Stick your nose inside, smell the possibilities! Inhale the hypnotic aroma of sex!

"Next. You. Lick the labia. Lick outside and then inside the cunt. Bury your tongue in there and feel the heat, the suppleness, the perfection.

"Next. You. Stick your finger up that cunt. Push it all the way up! Feel that spongy wall. Ah, that is the opening of the cervix. The *os* – the *mouth*! Now, pump your finger all the way in and all the way out. Good. Yes. See how the flesh writhes against you!

"Next. Suck on the pussy. Suck out all the thick, gooey ooze that gushed forth from the finger-fucking! Yes! Now search for the clitoris with your fingers and your mouth, and when you find it, kiss it and play with it with your tongue; rub it with your fingers.

"Next. Ah, Jet. Don't be shy! Step right up! Remember, Father knows best! Come on, that's right, boy. I will guide your pecker towards the mother cunt. That's right. Good. Slide the head of your engorged organ up and down inside the succulent labia. Yes! Now search out the clitoris with your prick. Good. Now, circle the entrance to the cunt with the head of your prick. Very good. Now we're going to enter slowly. You're in position. Push slightly. Good. Just the head inside the hole. Easy. Slowly. Gently. A little more. A little more. Perfect! Now, hold very still. Feel how the vagina grips the penis! Ahh. Close your eyes, all of you. Feel the hunger, the lust, the desire to fulfill your nature – the desire to *fill* the infinite nature!

"Now push further. One inch. Good. Hold still. Breathe. Now look at the archetypal nipples. See how hard they are, how the breasts rise and fall rapidly. Mother wants more! Give her more! Yes, that's good. Two inches. Hold still. Feel the energy. Hear the sound of your passion – your moaning, her panting. Ah, there is nothing but this moment! But you are greedy, you want more. You want to give her more. But wait, there's one thing more!

"Hurricane. Come. Look at the most powerful muscle in the human body! No, not the biceps or the thighs. The gluteus maximus. The ass! Look at it! The anus, the rectum – a short, muscular tube with two rings of muscle that encircle the one-and-one-half inch long anus. At the bottom of the rectum is a canal, and there you will find the internal anal sphincter on the inside and the external anal sphincter below it. And these rings are normally contracted – but it is possible to relax the muscles to open the end of the anal canal and enter the inner rectum. Go ahead, boy, get that ass ready to be fucked. Moisten the opening. Work your tongue into the tight hole. Use your finger. Yes. That's good. Now two fingers. Good. Daisy, come. Suck my dick! Oh, yes, my good child.

"Now, gather closer, children. Listen how your Mother begs for more! Oh, yes! That's right! I'll give you more, bitch! Come, children! Watch as your father fucks your mother. See in your mind's eye a battery of consecrated motile spermatozoon soldiers, supercharged, advancing, blades at the ready, bursting to unload into this juicy dripping hole and penetrate the walls of the ovum! Oh, the sacred stuff of our future is about to erupt! Oh yes! That's right. Say it with me: *Fuck that cunt, Daddy! Fuck that cunt, Daddy!* Say it! Oh, yes! That's good! Now, count with me! *One, two* . . .

■ ■ ■

Sounds of flesh slapping against flesh. *Yes. Oh, God. More. Harder. Faster. Slower. Wider. Yes! Yes! Yes!* Sounds of *Sgt. Pepper, Exile on Main Street, Nevermind,* Led Zeppelin, Jimi Hendrix, Janis Joplin, *Joshua Tree.* Taste of dried fungi. Smell of rank sex. Inhalation of whippits (we are *nitheads!*) and, oh, yes, our favorite, Special-T! and . . .

. . . They love me *and* they love my ink! I love them and theirs. I want that same wavy black line tattooed on my arm. I want to be just like them! They are happy and naked and dancing – one mass of flaming fusible flesh groovin' to the beat in a small wooden bungalow with undulating walls! And I'm on fire too. And I'm naked too. And I'm dancing and prancing with them – strutting my stuff across the floor – like "The Lips" himself! And we can hardly hear each other over the music. And I think sweet sexy Daisy shouts something to me but I'm not sure, so I just smile at her, and she smiles back and anyway it's all OK! We don't need words to commune! Our bodies are open! Our minds are open!

I close my eyes and twirl and twirl. I'm as dizzy as Gillespie! The amp blasts "The Boss" and I think, *Yes, I was Born to Run!* And I run around the room. And suddenly I realize something. *My limp is gone!* I run again, just to make sure. *It's a miracle! I've been cured!*

"Holy bat trap," I shout, "I'm healed!" I look around; no one hears me.

I look for Creed: *Where are you, my Healer, my Sister Aimee, my Kathryn Kuhlman?* I have to tell him *I'm a Believer*! I look everywhere. I can't find him. He's gone. And . . .

. . . Outside, the earth is moving. I can feel it under my feet. I put my head to the ground. I can hear them. I can hear the bodies rolling beneath the surface. The rolling bodies are dead but rapturous. *Aha! I get it! I finally understand! These are the Holy Rollers, rolling their way to the Promised Land! It's all so clear! Oh, how I'd like to join them, but I can't. Not now. Now, I have something else I must do – find the man in the long black coat.*

Lights coming from the other side of the hill are shining into the black night. It could be the main house. It could be the Mother Ship! The wet ground oozes up between my toes. If I stand in one spot too long I'll start growing roots – like a tree – and become fixed and immobile. No, I've got to keep moving. I wrap my arms around myself and trot and nicker like a wild colt. The air is cold, but I'm not. I'm hot and vibrating. I'm tingling all over. I'm alert and sharp-eyed as a hawk. And when the breeze comes it feels like tiny fingers tickling my bare flesh, and I giggle, which is funny because I'm not ticklish . . . but I am: *I am ticklish!* This makes me wonder about the millions of things I think I am not, but actually am. And this astounding and profound thought makes me laugh nervously. And when I laugh, multi-colored geometric shapes float out of my mouth, then burst like bubbles. I am high as the sky and getting higher by the second.

As I move further away from the revelry I start to hear something. It's foreign. I've never heard it before. I stop. What is it? I listen. Well, hot damn! Could it be? Is it? *Impossible.* I listen harder. And sure enough . . . it's not impossible! It could be! It is! It's the sound of silence! Silence inside my head! No noise. No incessant babble, no flapping tongue. No screaming, no begging. No analyzing, defining, judging. No measuring the depth of my pain or the fouling that left me unhinged. No, nothing. Bupkis! I can't believe it! It's all gone! Suddenly I feel strange. There's something in my body – it's filling me up, like water in an empty glass. Soon it's coursing through my veins . . . saturating my brain . . . and I am consumed and intoxicated. And when the vessel is full, I get it: *Love is silence! Silence is love! Wow.* And then out of nowhere I think: *There is no difference between irreverence and reverence!* I'm as deep as Groucho Marx on acid! Far fucking out.

The dirt road is steep, rocky. But I don't feel any pain cuz I don't have bare feet, I have hooves! I'm a horse, white and beautiful, and . . . I have wings! *I'm not just the Phoenix rising: I'm fucking Pegasus!* I fly to the top of the hill and spread my wings. I say hello to the passing trees and bushes and small furry creatures and they say *Welcome home, Honey!* Oh, I'm home! I'm one with the universe! I throw back my head and whinny. I feel so awake. I've never felt so awake.

From the top of the hill I look down. There is no Mother Ship. The lights are coming from the main house of the W.A.V.E.S. ranch, and the mad genius of the Fourth Wave is leaning against a car, legs outstretched. My heart goes thump, thump, thump. There's a woman with him. She's moving back and forth in front of him – her movements entertainingly exaggerated. I want to swoop down on them. I can hardly wait to tell him! Everything! My leg! My wings! My realizations! I can hardly wait to tell him he is right! I believe! I'm finally awake! I'm chomping at the bit and about to take wing, but something stops me . . .

. . . I'm flat on my belly. I'm not mythological anymore; I'm prehistoric. I'm small, reptilian, and quiet as a mouse. My legs and arms are scratched and bleeding from thistles and cacti, which I slithered through to avoid being seen. Now I'm close enough to see them, but they can't see me: I'm hidden behind a thicket. My senses are sharply tuned, superhuman. I can smell them – a pungent mixture of intimacy and anger, fear and conspiracy. I can hear them – his voice cocksure; her voice self-conscious. I can see them – every last detail – down to the color of the woman's flaming red hair.

"I can't!" Maggie says, stomping her foot.

"You will," he says.

She shakes her head, disagreeing.

"Come back tomorrow for the newsletters. Bring the money."

"Come with me now, *please*," she takes hold of his hands and goes down on her knees.

"I can't do that."

"*Why?* You've been doing it for years! *Why not now?* You'll be back before dawn."

"You know why."

Maggie stands and kicks the dirt.

"You're really enjoying your little *project*, aren't you?"

He doesn't care to answer.

"*What?!* You have to have *relations* with her twenty-four hours every day?!"

He gently pushes the red hair away from her eyes.

"Remember, my little Magpie. I wouldn't have this little *project* if you—"

"Oh, don't be so cruel! If I could have babies, you know I would, but—"

"You can't."

She looks up at the sky, heaves a big sigh, walks around in a little circle, then stops in front of him.

"Why did you have to pick . . . *her?*"

He takes his time answering. "Because . . . *she's the one.*"

"She's one foul-mouthed, smart-aleck, drunken blasphemer – that's what she is!"

"You only see the obvious. I don't have that limitation. I see the obscure. I comprehend the incomprehensible. I see light in the shadows. I see not just what lives, but what *survives*. Honey is a survivor. And she's . . . *unformed. Moldable.* She suits my purpose. She is useful. I am shaping her," he laughs maniacally. "And she is fecund. And I am pollinating, fertilizing, inseminating, and sanctifying her sperm-sucking corpus with a constant profusion of providential pus!"

Maggie starts to cry. Creed grabs her shoulders and shakes her violently.

"Get control of yourself! You are the First Wife of the Creed of Kurgan, woman! Don't forget that! And don't forget: this foul-mouthed, smart-aleck, drunken blasphemer, as you call her, will bear *your* progeny!"

"I'm sorry," she sobs.

He pulls her close and wraps his arms around her.

"Now. Tell me about the Ochs family. They still in town?"

She nods into his chest.

"Irony brings a deep but unfriendly understanding of life."

She nuzzles him, but doesn't respond.

"Still talking to Dunk?"

She nods again.

"What're they talking about?"

"You know the Marshal. Doesn't like to be questioned, and doesn't like questioners."

"Funny. I was certain no one would miss her," he says, as if talking to himself. "I was certain no one would care. She's a loner, an outsider: mother-less, fatherless, family-less, friendless, homeless. Drastic times call for drastic measures. I took drastic measures to ensure that she had no way out – that she could never – would never – leave here."

"She couldn't get out if she tried," she says. "This place is a fortress."

"I didn't anticipate this . . . Skinner Ochs," he says, ignoring her comment. "How could I?" He laughs again, like a madman.

"I'm worried."

He pushes her back.

"Don't worry. The boy will be on his way soon enough. He didn't come for her. Why would he? Unless . . . the little temptress. But, I doubt that. He wouldn't commit adultery."

"How would you know?"

"Just guessing – based on what I've heard. Benezer says his wife is particu-larly . . . *appealing*. So, why would Skinner be tempted by some gimpy misfit?"

He laughs. Maggie shakes her head.

"I don't know—"

"Oh, stop your worrying. Pie Town is just a courteous accommodation between law enforcement officials that ended up being the first stop on a family vacation. And, if it turns out different . . . well, we'll just wait and see which way the cat jumps. But don't you worry. I'll take care of everything. I always do, don't I?"

He kisses Maggie's forehead, pushes her brusquely, and opens the car door.

"Who's clerking the post office?"

"Fob Johnson," she says softly.

"Fob. Widower. Two boys. Interesting. His youngsters close to Benezer?"

"They attend his Bible meetings. The minister is helping the boys – all the kids – cope with their loss. They got awfully scared after . . . after what happened to their friend, Rabbit."

"Benezer will teach them to trust the Prophet. And, as long as they keep the covenant – the secret – as long as they don't betray my trust, they have nothing to fear."

Creed helps Maggie into the car.

"Did Rabbit betray your trust?" she asks meekly.

Creed holds onto the door frame and bends down so's they're face-to-face.

"Benezer had invested years priming Rabbit for the Fourth Wave, as he does all our young neophytes. The time had come, and I was prepared to reveal myself to Rabbit and welcome him into the amplitude. He was just weeks away from full induction. But he stuck his nose where it didn't belong. Yes! He betrayed God's trust. Unfortunate for him. Good for me – as it turned out." He laughs and kisses her forehead. "We must be willing to sacrifice for the cause . . . even our own lives."

"What about Daisy? You know how she loves Rabbit – how she's been waiting for him to come. Does she know? What did you tell her?"

"You think I can't handle some witless little girl's puppy love?" He laughs and pats Maggie's head like she's a dog. "Leave Daisy to me." He kisses her hand. "Now go. Tell Benezer to drop the newsletters off at the post office personally. I want to start sending the mail through again – the sooner, the better. The letters keep the unbelievers from asking questions and getting funny ideas into their heads – like trying to locate their children. Tell Benezer to chat up old Fob. Take his temperature, drop the lure. If nothing else, man needs a vessel. Tell the minister to dangle the young, juicy bait . . . all the pubescent pussy the old man could ever want . . . free for the taking! If he's man enough, he'll join us. If we can reel Fob in, his boys will follow. The apple doesn't fall far from the tree!" He laughs crazily. "Now, don't forget what I'm telling you."

"I won't," she says sweetly.

He stands up.

"Come back tomorrow, after midnight, for the newsletters. Don't forget the money."

"OK."

He slams the car door shut. She starts the engine.

"Did Benezer sell the Javelin?"

"Yes, to a collector."

"What did he get for it?"

"Seventy-five hundred."

"That's disappointing."

"The collector agreed to pay twelve, but when he saw that the original paint job had been redone he—"

"I see. He paid cash."

"Yes."

"Good. That's ten AK-47s, and a new shipment from Cyprus! I've got a new contact. Looks very promising. Don't forget. Bring the cash tomorrow."

She starts to pull back, but stops and sticks her head out.

"Sure you won't come with me?" she asks suggestively.

He isn't tempted.

"I love you, Tommy."

The taillights disappear down the road. The man turns, wild-eyed. He hotfoots it into the woods – toward the orgiastic wingding of intoxicated flesh awaiting his return. And my mind opens so wide that my brain falls right out.

■ ■ ■

Tommy? I love you, Tommy? No. That can't be. That's not Tommy. That's Creed Kurgan, the Prophet. I must've heard wrong. Maybe she said, "I love you, honey." Yeah, that must be it. But that would mean that the God-fearing Maggie Horton was cheating on her poor crippled husband, which would make the God-fearing Maggie Horton a low-down slutty hosebag. No, not Maggie! But . . . maybe she wasn't *cheating. Maybe she took the Prophet home for some freaky sex-capades with her* and *Tommy. Or maybe poor Tommy, being paralyzed and all, got off by watching. Or? Did he say she was the first wife of Creed Kurgan? That would mean God-fearing Maggie Horton wasn't cheating cuz she had two husbands.*

Oh, it hurt to think. But I couldn't stop.

I mean, what about poor little Daisy, pining for her dead white Rabbit? Puppy love harmless? Two names: Starkweather and Fugate. Oh, Skinner. Am I in puppy love with you? Were you tempted by a gimpy-misfit-with-an-unformed-moldable-fecund-sperm-sucking-corpus?

■ ■ ■

I can't trust my eyes or my ears. The holy sacrament is making me see things, hear things, perceive things that aren't real. Maybe the woman's hair was brown. Maybe there was no woman. I can't be sure of anything. Except . . . well . . . there is one thing. One thing I *feel* . . . unquestionably. It's raw and primal and intense. And it can be summed up in a one-syllable word with four letters: F-E-A-R.

The heavy door creaks open and I creep down wooden planked stairs. It's dark, cold, silent. I feel blindly along the walls. A single switch. Minimal light. A cavernous room, stone walls, concrete floor. I press along the walls, sidle past an enormous printing press – *the source of the thumping?* – to a narrowing corridor that goes pitch-black within a foot of its gaping curved entrance. A shiver runs down my spine: *Hellsmouth*. Technicolor hallucinations. *The Leviathan*. Bad trip. Bad trip. *Creed . . . er, Tommy? . . . and . . . Maggie?*

I press against the wall. I need to be something solid, something unbroken. My body has fragmented into a million tiny pieces, suspended gravity-free just out of reach. I can't think straight. Panic. *I gotta get outta this place, if it's the last thing I ever do*. Nervous laugh.

I snake along the wall and around a corner to a hallway. There are several doors; one is open. I look behind me. I hear something. My heart pounds; sweat rolls down my face. *If he catches me I'm dead. Maybe I'm dead already*. I tiptoe into the room and lurch. My limp is back. *Once I was healed, but now I'm fucked*. I hear footsteps; I feel someone's hot breath on my neck. My heart stops. *It's just the mushrooms*, I tell myself. I turn on a small lamp. Metal industrial bookcases holding identically sized black notebooks, uniformly labeled, numerically arranged. The desk, partly hidden beneath masses of meticulously stacked papers. No telephone, no computer. My leg buckles. I hold onto the cold metal desk and edge my way around. I sit in the metal chair – cold against my hot naked flesh. I rummage drawers. Documents in foreign languages. Transcriptions. Bills of lading. Ledgers. Invoices. Catalogs. Catalogs of weapons: assault rifles, handguns. And then, a small silver handgun in my palm . . . spongy and warm, like a soft-boiled egg. *Gadzooks!* It disintegrates and disappears. Letters. Hundreds of letters. Groups of letters banded together – addressed to Alice Guthrie, Pop and Josie Clover, Caudill Jackson. *The missing letters.* Everything wants to fall into place, but can't. Thoughts distort and mutate, become unrecognizable. Brain synapses communicate a language without words – an assault of persuasive delusion, extreme color, consuming sensation.

Next door, heavy, stone. Guns. Guns everywhere. Big. Small. Boxes and boxes of ammunition. Hand grenades. Tear gas. Bazookas. *Bazookas?* Enough hardware to supply an army: the Army of Creed Kurgan.

Next door, heavy, stone. Gigantic room. *Warehouse?* An ocean of boxes – plastic-strapped together, stacked, towering, five feet above my head. I limp up and down the aisles, run my hand along the boxes. My hand passes right through the cardboard; I'm a ghost. I stop and look at labels. Foreign. Italian. Spanish. French. Latin. I don't know. *It's all Greek to me.* Nervous laugh.

Next door, heavy, stone. Post office. Envelopes addressed and heaped in Out box. The postmark: a wavy line above barely legible letters, with a solid black line beneath. I stare. The barely legible letters turn into dots. My mind connects them with a pencil-thin line: W-A-V-E-S – *World Advocacy for Values in an Enlightened Society*, I think by rote. My mind is blown, and W-A-V-E-S start to swell and roll and I get seasick and upchuck a thick stream of greenish-black slime. Chunks of it land on my breasts and belly and the rest lands on my bare feet. I get down on hands and knees and examine the slime carefully: maybe it contains important information. It doesn't. Nervous laugh.

I've got to get out. But how? *Didn't the redhead say the place was a fortress? Was she a redhead? I'm not sure. Maybe. Maybe not. OK. Maybe someone will come looking for me. Didn't the man say Skinner wasn't looking for me? Didn't he say no one was looking for me? Maybe the woman who wasn't Maggie and wasn't a redhead didn't call Creed Tommy. Maybe the man who wasn't Tommy wasn't even Creed.* Fuck.

I skulk towards the stairs and then I see it, positioned at the end of the printing press. I walk over and stare. It's the front page of this week's edition of *The Fourth Wave*, ready to roll. The plate starts to undulate; the letters float off the page. Fuck. I've had enough of the "sacrament." I want my brain back. I look away and back again. It reconstitutes itself. I pick up a nearby mat knife and etch a couple of changes into the front right corner. Maybe the fella who does the thumping won't notice. Maybe someone else will.

■ ■ ■

I sit on a mound of pine needles, hidden from the road. The wind doesn't tickle anymore. My teeth clatter. My body is heavy. Moving is a struggle – like swimming upstream against a current of thick lava. But if I hold still my limbs take root, burrowing deeply into the cold damp earth. There are monsters everywhere.

I close my eyes and tell myself it's the psilocybin – it'll wear off soon enough. But it doesn't, and my mind continues to drift in and out of far-out realities, and I slowly start to obsess about extraterrestrials – and I start to see extraterrestrials. And I start to believe that *I* am an ET. And suddenly lightning strikes in the distant fields and when I look up I see two large white orbs. They're moving towards me! *The Mother Ship!* Yes! This time it *is* the Mother Ship! And it's coming for me!

I try to get up but I'm weighted down by the cold heavy metal thing in my lap: the gun. *How did it get there?* I pull myself up the trunk of the tree and look up. The lights are moving closer! I don't have much time! I've got to hide the gun! The aliens might be afraid! They might think I want to harm them! I look closely at the tree. Its branches are loaded with big red balls. I reach up and pluck one. A pomegranate! A perfectly round red pomegranate! I recognize it! I feel it! I have no doubt! I'm saved! I kiss the pomegranate and set it and the weapon in the bark-branch ridge, and then I look for the orbs. They're getting closer still. This is it! This is my way out! *The Mother Ship is coming to rescue me!* I run like a lubber towards the lights, my arms raised high above my head, flailing wildly. The lights grow bigger. I get closer! They get closer! They're so close, I'm blinded! I stand like a crucifix, my arms straight out in a tee, my legs spread, my naked tattooed body on full display, my hair standing straight up from the wind, and I close my eyes and yell, *Beam me up, Scotty!*

The door clanged open and shut. My eyes slowly adjusted to the darkness. Creed stood over me. He stared down, unblinking. His gaze was cold – his body still, solid, immovable – like a mountain that had endured despite years of punishing wind and rain. He didn't move and he didn't blink and his expression didn't change. He just stood there and gave me the dead-eye. *The calm before the storm*. Minutes passed. I lowered my head. I felt raw, vulnerable, sapped. I was just back from Magic Mushroom Land – and the trip had been . . . fucking exhausting.

"It was an accident. You ran out into the road. We didn't have time to stop. You've got cuts and bruises. A few broken ribs. Dr. Cocker bandaged you up. Says you'll survive."

He paused long enough for my memory to return. *Two white orbs rocketing towards me. Landing lights of an alien spacecraft. But wait. No. They're too small to be landing lights. They're . . . headlights. Two headlights . . . attached to . . . the grill of a fast-moving truck. A deadening thud. Then darkness.* Suddenly my body was racked with pain. Suddenly it hurt to breathe. I gasped and winced.

"You shouldn't have tried to get away from me," he smiled menacingly. "*Big* mistake."

A shiver of dread ran through my body. I closed my eyes and wrapped my arms around my ribs, trying to stop the pain and escape the reality of impending doom.

"I was . . . confused . . . the mushrooms . . . fungal . . . I think, I . . . I mean, I think you . . . I mean, I thought . . . I think . . ." I stammered incoherently, trying to sound contrite.

He gave me a quick, sharp kick to the ribs – the broken ribs. I squealed and wheezed, curling up into a tight little ball on the cold damp floor.

"Thinking is highly overrated, *especially in your circumstances.*"

"What are my . . . *circumstances?*" I forced weakly through the pain.

He gave me another kick.

"Stop! Please! I . . . I didn't know what I was doing! Please, don't hurt me."

"I could have dropped you off on Marshal Hayward's doorstep. You and the murder weapon – the one you used to kill Rabbit Rawlings – the one with yours and Rabbit's bloody fingerprints on it. I could have turned you in. But . . ." he paused and made a growling sound, "I have *other* plans for you. Bigger plans!"

"Just kill me now and get it over with," I sniveled softly.

He laughed sadistically.

"Ha! You'd like that, wouldn't you? The easy way out. No! No more easy way out for you! There's a price to pay for disobeying Daddy, and you're going to pay it."

"Please, Daddy."

"You'll thank me later, Jezebel!"

"When monkeys fly out of my ass," I hissed mockingly.

He stared at me with daggers, then smiled.

"Suffer, monkey, suffer!" he shouted viciously.

He gave me another sharp kick to the head. I yelped and saw stars.

"You've been a *very* bad girl. Very naughty."

"I won't . . . do it . . . again," I stuttered, writhing in pain.

The iron door clanged open and shut. Keys rattled. He locked the cell door. Then he was gone.

I lay on the cold dirt floor, twisting in pain, shivering. I clutched a small scratchy blanket against my naked body, as if it would protect me from harm. But I knew it wouldn't. I knew there would be no protection: the worst was yet to come. I'd felt hopeless before; I'd felt dread – lots of times. But never like this. I'd talked about wanting to die, but I never really meant it . . . maybe this time would be the exception.

I tried to will the pain into submission. I tried to quiet the fear. I pictured good ole Alice telling me to keep my pecker up. I pictured her picking up a copy of *The Fourth Wave* at the post office and noticing a queer little chicken scratch in the upper right corner and knowing that it was a message from me to her. Just thinking about the good-natured wide-assed gal who'd put me on her list eased the pain some. But thinking about all the nasty things I'd done with her boys, well, it made me upchuck, which sent my pecker right back down.

Well, this is a fine mess you've gotten us into. A short anxious sound escaped my mouth, and then I drifted off into blackness.

I woke up to clanging and the sound of footsteps. I watched shadows cast by flickering light dance along the stone wall outside my cell. *The Mountain was back.* And he had reinforcements. *Fuck.*

He unlocked the cell and moved towards me. He stood me up, and held me up – one hand clenching the scruff of my neck. He ripped the ratty blanket from my hand. He applied red lipstick to my lips, then smeared it across my face with the back of his hand. He held me aside so's Hurricane and Snake and Patience and Daisy could enter. Without instruction, they set their candlesticks around me in a circle and knelt at his feet.

"Woman is the origin of sin, and it is through her that we will die . . . *unless* she is re-formed," he said calmly.

Fear shot through my aching body.

"*Please—*" I begged.

He shook me violently, rattling my piteous little brain.

"A willful woman is a shameless bitch! Wherefore, my beloved Honey, you have obeyed me not, I will teach you compliance! By fire you will learn! But do not fear or tremble for what you are about to suffer. Be faithful unto death!"

He threw me down, putting his boot on my shoulder to keep me on my back. I heard a whipping sound before I saw the whip. I felt a sting across my face and tasted blood in my mouth.

"I offer you salvation! I offer you redemption – the return of the chaste feminine principle – just as nature intended it! And this is how you repay me! Instead of submission, you give me defiance!"

Before I could plead for mercy he raised the leather strap again and in one quick movement thrashed a line straight down the center of my naked body. The pain was exquisite – something beyond. The incision was perfect: a straight slit of trauma to my flesh, half an inch deep. Salty stinging tears flowed into the gutter of exposed tissue on my face. The genuflecting amplitude began to sob. Suddenly, it all seemed funny, and I started to laugh.

"I am consumed by anger! And by defiance I am troubled! Her iniquities are before me; her secret sins are in the light of my countenance!"

"*Yippee yi-o ki-a motherfucker!*" I shouted hysterically.

He raised the strap and thrashed me again with the same speed and exactness, and when he was through slicing me vertically he opened me up horizontally, and when he finished with the front of my body he flipped me over and repeated the precise operation to my back.

Daisy wrapped herself around his legs like a humping dog and pleaded with him to stop. He shook her loose, and she fell next to me.

"The disciple is never above her master! Nor the servant above her lord! Watch lest you be next, child!"

I reached out and put Daisy in a headlock. She screamed and struggled to get free. Creed roared with laughter. The believers started to yell. The room got very noisy. I took the chance, cupping my hands around her ear so's only she could hear. "Rabbit's dead. He killed him. There's a loaded gun in the pomegranate tree." I let her go and fell back, drained of all strength. She looked at me fearfully, wiped my blood off her face, and scampered off to a corner. It was so very noisy. *Did she hear what I said?*

"Silence, everyone!" Creed ordered. Then to me he bellowed, "I am the Savior! And you will bow under my feet! On your hands and knees!"

I was too weak to comply. He turned me over and twisted my broken bloody body into position. I collapsed like a rag doll. He grabbed me around the middle and pulled me back into position.

"'*Who can find a virtuous woman? Her price is far above rubies. The heart of her husband doth safely trust in her.*'"

With his free hand he unzipped his pants.

"'*She will do him good and not evil all the days of her life.*'"

He plunged into me in one forceful thrust.

"You are a willful bitch, but you *will* be my servant! I *will* fuck the Jezebel out of you!"

He fucked me hard. While ramming in and out, he reached around and began manipulating my clitoris. *Crazy motherfucker! Did he actually think he was gonna pleasure me now? What a sick fuck.* After a couple of minutes he bayed and pulled out abruptly, flinging me onto my back. He put one knee on each of my bent arms, pushed his pelvic forward, and jizzed all over my face, hollering, "*You will be purified! You will be re-formed! You will be my Vestal Virgin! Your sins were more than you could bear! I have taken your sins from you! You have been forgiven!*"

Within moments I was alone again, locked in the cell.

Funny, I didn't feel forgiven. I felt guilty, cuz I *was* guilty. My sins *were* more than I could bear. And not just cuz I was worthless and contemptible, a coward and a liar and a killer who had no right to be among the living. But cuz *just now* – though I'd been degraded, defiled, chastised, terrorized, and imprisoned, and though I'd been beaten and sliced open from head to toe, and even though a maniacal-homicidal-sadistic-manny-jamming-Manson-wannabe cuntophile had raped me – I *had* been pleasured – I had given up my Big O. It had happened against my will, because I had no will.

They gave me a horse hypo of analgesic and hooked me up with Special-T. They spoon-fed me Creed's cum from a nice shiny bowl. They licked my wounds – face, eyes, mouth, nose, ears, neck, breasts, ribs, belly, pelvis, pussy, legs, thighs, feet, toes. At first I resisted: it was hard to think for the pain, but if I *was* gonna think, and come up with a plan to escape the Prophet of Bunkum and his androids, I needed to stay sober. But after a while . . . well . . . the dope took over, and I slid into an agreeable stupor where I felt less – less pain, less fear, less urgency. *Why not look on the bright side? After all, shit happens. Plus, things could always be worse. Why be a Debbie Downer?*

I let them soothe me, work me over – front and back. We were a pack of wild animals; they were tending to the one who'd been caught by the predator. They were saving me, healing me. I joined in, licking the gash on my forearm. The bloody innards of raw flesh tasted dirty and gritty, yummy in a gamy way. They gave me more dope. And when I half-heartedly asked where Daisy was, they just cooed and caressed and continued to lick, and my token curiosity quickly morphed from *Did Daisy believe me? Did she even hear what I said about Rabbit? Did she find the pomegranate tree and the gun?* to: *Daisy* who?

Hours later Doc Cocker and Maggie came into the cell. He carried a medical bag and a full-length mirror; she brought candles and an armload of fabric. My lickers stood and left quietly and quickly. Then Creed entered. The three of them hovered.

"She must be circumcised," Creed stated, matter-of-factly.

I must be *what*? "Hey . . . hold on . . . just a sec," I said weakly.

"She needs more time," Cocker said, ignoring my words and looking over my naked, wounded body.

"*No more time!* Skinner Ochs is still in Pie Town, asking questions. The investigation could lead to—"

"You don't have to worry, Tommy. He's leaving tomorrow. Their car is already packed. Alice told me they're just waiting on daylight," Maggie said surely.

"If that's the case, then why rush?" Cocker reasoned. "I'd really feel much better if—"

"*No!* The Creed of Kurgan – the Fourth – and *final* – Wave has waited for millennia! I won't wait any longer! Salvation must come from a virgin womb! It's the only path! She must be *cut* in order to be purified!"

"But I've never performed female . . . *circumcision* . . . before. I need more time. It's complicated. Dangerous. I need to do more research—"

"Don't give me that namby-pamby bullshit! The procedure has been done since the time of the Pharaohs! It's done every day in Asia and Africa! It couldn't be simpler! You sterilize your instruments, give her anesthesia, cut off her clitoris and the labia minora, then stitch the vulva together to cover the vagina. Instant virgin! Vestal Virgin! *My* Vestal Virgin! When I come to procreate with her I will unstitch the vessel and re-stitch it when I have finished. It will increase my pleasure ten-fold. That will increase my desire to procreate! Yes! Our progeny will be prolific! Our future lies in her virgin womb! What could be simpler?!"

Oh, gee, let me think. I tried to make a suggestion but no words came out.

"I don't know," he said, bending down to inject another horse hypo of knock-out narcotics into my body. "It's risky in her weakened condition."

"Tommy, if the doctor says—"

"Shut up, woman!" Creed yelled. He slapped Maggie's face and she started to sob.

They're talking about mutilating my *little kitty, and* she's *the one crying?*

"You have taken an oath to the Creed of Kurgan! You *will* do as I say, Cocker," Creed threatened.

Cocker gave Maggie a "can't you reason with him?" look. But she just held her cheek and whimpered. The doctor frowned and rubbed his forehead. Creed paced, then came to a sudden stop.

"A lab rat! That's what you need. I'll get you one. She may not have a virgin womb, but she'll do for our purpose."

The doctor stopped frowning and the red-head stopped crying, and they looked at Creed quizzically.

"No questions! Leave it to me. In the meantime, prepare! And remember: *you* are my redeemers! You are among the elite, and will be remembered throughout history! You are Kurgan warriors! It was the Kurgan warriors who first understood the active and passive principles of creation – the upper and lower waters – the "male" and female" forces. It was the *Kurgan* warrior who brought order to chaos! It was *our* ancestors who swarmed down on the continent to right the course of humanity! The battle rages on! And this time we will prevail!"

Maggie Horton and Joe Cocker stood mesmerized, all the fight gone from their faces. I was barely conscious. But still – drugged, wounded, defeated, despoiled, desecrated, and/or otherwise self-hating – I formed a thought: I'd drunk the Kool-Aid cuz I figured, well, what did I have to lose other than my worthless life? Now I knew the answer: *my clit*. And that was *not* gonna happen. And if I could've opened my mouth and said so, I would've said so right then and there.

"I'll put her in a drug-induced coma. I'll give her IV antibiotics. In a week she'll be strong as an ox."

"You've got two days. I don't need an ox," Creed laughed madly. "I need a lamb."

The pain woke me. Sharp. Burning. Head to toe. I winced and let out a clipped yelp. *Take short shallow breaths, Honey – till the hurting stops.* But how long would that be? I didn't know. I didn't know anything. I couldn't remember where I was or how I got here. I was teetering on a thin edge somewhere between consciousness and hallucination – my thoughts all tangled up – nothing taking root, nothing making sense.

My swollen eyes slowly adjusted to the darkness, and by bits and pieces things came into focus. The cold dirt floor, the windowless room, the iron bars. A disconnected IV taped to the vein on the top of my hand – the hand with four-and-a-half fingers. I started to bawl outright. I hated myself for what I'd done. What *had* I done? Oh, God. Suddenly the whole sordid story started to crash over me, unstoppable as a tsunami: *The man in the long black coat . . . the sex . . . the dead bodies . . . the madness . . .*

I ran my fingers over my face. I was all cut up – deep precise cuts, criss-crossing my face vertically and horizontally. Some were crusted over, some still oozing. Creed had been meticulous in his work: my face had been turned into a goddamn grid, a game board, a map. I looked down at my body. It was the same. Cut up. Bruised. Some parts naked and exposed, some parts covered loosely in bloody gauze. *Fuck.* I'd been invaded, savaged, slaughtered. And yet somehow I was still alive – still a survivor. *Why? Why couldn't I just fucking die already?*

I heard a noise coming from behind me. A groan. A man's groan. *Oh, God.* I turned slightly. In the back corner I saw a shape – a large black shape, curled up in the fetal position. He groaned again. *Oh, God. I'm not alone in this cell!*

Get a grip, gal. Get a grip. Think. Think. Yeah, I got it: things could always be worse. Somewhere at this very moment a beautiful brokenhearted woman is taking a lethal dose of sleeping pills in the backseat of her car and jotting down her last broken words in a note addressed to the man who did her in. *But then again, things could always be better.* Somewhere at this very moment a ninety-to-one long-shot named Foxy Gerry was crossing the finish line at Belmont, delivering to some lucky loser – who'd bet his last fifty bucks on the mare – the biggest payday of his life.

Yeah, that's right, Honey. Things are always going from better to worse and back again.

But right then, as I placed the face that went with the sounds of misery coming from behind me, there was no getting around it: things had gone from worse straight to Hell.

I turned and looked at him: Skinner Ochs, in all his big beautiful glory, handcuffed by the arms and legs and hog-tied in the corner, trying to shake off whatever it was had knocked him for a loop.

I covered my face with my hands. I pressed my thumbs into my ears and jiggled fast so's I wouldn't hear his suffering. This couldn't be happening. I said *"no"* over and over and over again. I wormed my way into an opposite corner of the cell – snarling from the pain as I moved – and curled up into a tight little ball, my face hidden. But I couldn't escape. I could smell him. I could feel his bright baby blues looking at me – looking at me the way he always looked at me – with a true and innocent love. It was that look that drove me all the way to Pie Town.

"Of all the gin joints in all the towns in all the world . . ." he said haltingly.

I bit my lower lip and sobbed miserably. *Oh, sweet Skinner* – always so cool and easy – especially when the going got tough. I'd almost forgotten. Still, I couldn't stomach him seeing the mess I was – naked and beaten and sliced up. Even though his eyeglasses were lying broken across the room, he'd surely see that I wasn't exactly a fella's wet dream. Since the first day I met him he'd been the porn star of all my fantasies. But in all of them – from playing doctor to circle-jerk gangbang – I'd never imagined a picture like this.

"Please . . . don't look at me," I cried, burying my face in my hands.

"Sorry. Not possible, pardner," he muttered, pain in his voice.

I slowly uncurled, pulled myself up to a slumped sitting position, lowered my hands, and raised my head.

He squinted at me and cringed. The left side of his face twitched. *"Who . . . who did that to you?"* he asked, unable to check his horror.

I broke down, thick gobs of snot dangling from my chin.

"Hey, pardner, don't cry. I'd come over there, but . . ." He grunted and struggled against his shackles. "How about you come over here? Help me get loose."

I shut my eyes and shook my head. "This can't be happening," I said loudly. "This can't be happening," I repeated again and again.

"Honey! Honey! Don't check out on me now. Stay with me. I need you. This is push-come-to-shove time." He moaned in pain. "Awh. Come on, pardner. Let's put our heads together. We've been in tight spots before. We can figure this . . ." His voice trailed off. Then he said, "Mary." And then, "The girls."

I stopped. A cold shiver of dread shot through my body.

"Where are they? Mary. The girls."

I shrugged helplessly and shook my head.

"Last I remember . . . we were on the Interstate. Right. We were on the Interstate." He paused, as if struggling to remember what happened next. Then he said, "Right. We were twenty, thirty miles outside of Pie Town. There was a young woman broke down on the side of the road. She flagged us down." He paused again. Then he said, "Right. I told Mary and the girls to stay in the car. I went to look under the hood. A couple of guys came up from behind. Got the jump on me." Pause. "They must've knocked me out."

"Scumbags."

"Who are these people?"

"W.A.V.E.S. World Advocacy for Values in an Enlightened Society. It's some kind of . . . sect . . . or, I don't know. It's crazy. The fella who heads it is totally off his nut. I mean, "Redrum, redrum" bonkers. He thinks he's God, and he's got a whole bunch of other folks thinking it too. He's got some kind of insane plan to take over the world . . . or start a new society . . . I don't know, something. He's wacko, deranged. Name's Creed Kurgan or Tommy Horton or who knows what. Whatever. He's a sadistic woman-hating murderer – him and his *amplitude* – that's what he calls his followers – his *amplitude* – a bunch of brainwashed post-teens on magic mushrooms and happy gas. He killed – *they* killed – Rabbit Rawlings. They think I killed Rabbit, but it was them. And they killed the guard at the hospital. And poor Punchclock."

"Would they hurt Mary? The girls?"

I didn't wanna lie. I tried to think of something to say as the crushing horror of unspoken possibility sank in. My body shuddered and the cell grew ice-cold.

"They'd have no reason to hurt them," I managed meekly.

We sat in silence for a minute, then Skinner asked, "What are you doing here? Did he kidnap you? Did he kidnap these people?"

"No. Creed – or whatever – he's got *believers* in town. I don't know how many. The God-fearing Maggie Horton, definitely. She might even be married to the creep. The minister of Main Street Church, E. Benezer Stryker, for sure. I overheard a conversation. I picked up bits and pieces. It seems Stryker is chief of brainwashing. Uses his youth bible meetings as cover. Sounds like he starts in on them when they're real little and just keeps on them through high school graduation. Then, I guess, they're brought here to meet the Prophet – that's another one of his names. What a joke. Anyways, they come here, join their buddies, take an oath to Mr. Mad as a Hatter. It's all hush-hush – like a secret society, I guess. He publishes a newsletter called *The Fourth Wave*. They might have international connections. The parents of these droids are dumb as dirt – don't have any idea what's going on. Maybe they figure "What high school grad would wanna hang around Pie Town anyways?" so I guess it doesn't seem so strange when the kids hightail it outta town."

"So these kids come here of their own accord."

"They don't even know what their own accord is."

"What about you? I mean, no offense, but it seems out of character. You know who you are. You're strong, independent. It just doesn't make sense that you'd join some . . . cult . . . willingly."

"I didn't *join*. Not exactly." I sighed. *Did I really have to tell the X-rated truth? No.* "See, about a year ago I ran out of gas outside Pie Town, so I decided to hang my hat a spell, and then one night, well, I met this fella. This Creed Kurgan fella. By accident. And, well . . . he . . ." I was suddenly jolted by a high-speed trip down memory lane. I'd gone so far and sunk so low since that night.

"He what?"

He pushed my hand down his pants and wrapped it firmly around his hot swollen bozack. He squeezed and moved our hands together back and forth along the thick throbbing shaft and told me to say hello to Daddy. And boy, did I ever.

"He was kinda . . . interested. In me. And I guess I was needing some . . . attention . . . of the manly ilk." I hung my head.

"Like my pa always said, 'Be careful what you wish for.'"

I started to cry. *How long had it been since Skinner quoted me from his pa? It sure seemed like forever. But even in the hopelessness of his circumstances, I still heard it in his voice: pride – pride fashioned from the strong foundation upon which he stood . . . and a conviction about what was righteous and good in life.*

"Don't worry, pardner. We'll get out of this. Come over here."

I started to inch my way towards him. Maybe he was right. Maybe we could get out of this. But even if it was too late for me – even if I couldn't get out alive – I had to help him. After all, I owed him. In the first place, he'd taken a bullet to the head to save my life, and in the second, it was my fault he was in this fix in the first place. I'd help him escape. I'd find Mary and the girls. I'd do whatever it took. And I had a good idea that "whatever it took" was gonna get pretty fucking ugly – starting out with how I was gonna explain the sentimental words tattooed across my belly.

"Hang on," I said. "I'm coming."

"Hurry up."

"Hold your horses. I'm—"

I stopped talking, moving, breathing, and listened. Footsteps. Approaching.

"Oh, God, Skinner. They're coming," I whispered and started to tremble.

"Easy does it, pardner."

I lifted my head to the ceiling.

"Oh, God. Save him," I whispered.

Hurricane unlocked the cell and Creed entered. He was wearing a black robe with a hood covering all but a small part of his face. Jet, Melody, Patience, and Daisy followed. Creed nodded. Hurricane picked up the eyeglasses, dusted them off, put them on Skinner, checked the handcuffs, and tightened the ropes. Skinner protested, and Jet walked over and kicked him hard in the gut. Creed laughed insanely. Skinner stopped protesting. Creed waited, ready to direct his bum-boy to deliver another blow, but Skinner was still and silent. I knew he was hurt, but I also knew he was smart. I had to be smart too.

"Good morning, my sweet betrothed," Creed said cheerfully, turning his attention to me. "You must be starving."

He bent down and kissed me softly on the lips. I didn't resist. Then he signaled, and a large shiny bowl was handed to him.

"It wasn't easy to fill this large bowl," he teased. "But my girls here gave me a hand!" He looked at the girls; they blushed. "Now, Jezebel, open wide."

He pressed the bowl to my lips. I opened my mouth best I could. He slowly poured the thick fresh sticky cum into my mouth. It didn't go down. I couldn't swallow. It filled my mouth and then overflowed, stinging as it oozed into the cuts in my face. I heaved forward, retching and vomiting. Nothing came out.

"That's all right. You'll eat later," he said, giving me a patronizing "good dog" pat on the head. "Anyway, it's time to rise and shine! It's your big day!"

The Guthrie boys stood me up and dragged me to the mirror, which was leaning against the far wall. Melody unwrapped the few pieces of gauze from my body and lit a few candles. Then she joined the amplitude, who stood behind, blocking Skinner's view: a small mercy.

"Look," Creed said, as they held me up in front of the mirror.

I looked. Then I cried. Not tears of horror at the sight of my damaged, marked body. It was something else. It was . . . me. For the first time in my life, I saw myself.

"Honey," I said, blinking through my tears.

"Yes," Creed whispered.

Yes, I finally looked like on the outside what I felt like on the inside. I was fully exposed, sliced open from head to toe, and I wasn't repulsed by the reflection; I was awestruck, mesmerized. I recognized each and every gash, wound, scab, scar. I'd earned them. I deserved them.

"Honey," I said again, and the tears kept flowing, and the girls behind me started to sob softly.

I'd never really seen myself before – never. I had only seen the reflection of some gal I didn't recognize, a gal shaped from pain, a gal who moved through life like a scurrying rat trying to escape the foot of doom. And when I looked into the face of that gal, well, sometimes I'd recognized her broken heart and I'd known that her tears could fill an ocean. But those tears would have to wait! Cuz right then, standing in front of the mirror, with flesh hanging off my bones and bright red, blue, purple, green, and yellow bruise marks covering my body, I felt fearless and strong – almost beautiful. No, there was no mistaking it: the thin, deep, precise gashes that crisscrossed my body, the blood, the still readable tattoo, all of it – it was me, turned inside out. And I don't know, the simple genius of the moment just took my breath away, and for an instant I drifted off to a place where there was no more pain, and I felt only one thing: gratitude. Gratitude for life's small mercies. And I wondered, *Who do I thank for these rare and fleeting moments of clemency?* I'd have to remember to ask someone about that. And I knew just who that someone would be: Skinner P. Ochs, of course. Skinner Ochs. *Skinner:* the man hog-tied on the floor behind me. *Hello darkness my old friend . . .*

Creed caught me before I fainted and held me tightly in his arms. I wanted to push him away, but I didn't have the strength. Plus, I had to be clever. I had to stay sober and focused. I had to outsmart the man in the long black coat – the man who'd transformed me and made me see myself for who I really was – the man who now pushed one finger into my pussy and another into my booty.

As he finger-fucked me I thought about how much of Creed's cum was in my body, and wondered if it hadn't somehow re-formed me already. I thought about how badly I had wanted his cum inside of me – any way, any day. I thought about how something that I longed for once was now so repulsive. *Was it just cuz Skinner was here?* If he weren't here, would I be squirming and gyrating and begging for more? *No.* I didn't want Creed's cum anymore. I didn't want him inside me. And, you know, after everything was said and done, well, I just had to admit it: sometimes a great fuck just wasn't enough.

My big day.

I couldn't really appreciate the magic of the moment – not the way the freaks did. The girls were positively slap-happy, stoned out of their bufflebrains. They merrily handed me a wad of mushroom powder. When they weren't looking I dropped it and rubbed it into the dirt.

Skinner lay in the opposite corner, in a tight tortured ball. He seemed to be slipping in and out of consciousness, uttering an occasional painful moan. It was agony.

As soon as Creed and his boys left – so's my "attendants" could get me ready for my upcoming nuptials – I made my move.

"We've gotta get outta here," I said calmly – as they put ointment and gauze over my wounds.

Melody cooed and the other two ignored me and they all continued wrapping me up like a mummy.

"Listen to me," I whispered conspiratorially. "I was sent here on a mission… from the High Master . . . of the . . . New . . . Millennium. He sent me here to find you gals, and to take you to him."

They smiled understandingly.

"This is serious," I continued, seriously. "The High Master heard about the three of you. He mentioned you specifically, *by name!* He knows Creed Kurgan, and he told me to tell you that Creed Kurgan is a reincarnation of Ivan the Terrible and . . . Attila the Hun and . . . Genghis Khan and . . . Vlad the Impaler! He's merciless! He's a killer! Listen to me! You're in grave danger!"

I grabbed Daisy's arm. "He told me to tell you that Creed Kurgan murdered Rabbit Rawlings." Daisy yanked her arm from me. Although she kept smiling, I detected a hint of something in her eyes. *Did she find the pomegranate tree? The gun?* "The High Master told me to tell you that if you find anything in . . . in a tree, for instance . . . you should give it to me."

"Shhh, now," Melody chirped. "The Prophet says you need your strength for your . . . *wedding night.*"

The androids giggled like virgins – like they hadn't been partying hearty every fucking night all night long with Big Jim & The Twins.

"No can do," I said, firmly. "I've been sent for you, and if I fail – if *you* fail to come with me – then . . . then *blackness* will cover the earth!"

I nodded and squinted sinisterly. They stopped.

"That's right. *Blackness.* The apocalypse! The . . . the . . . "

"End of Days," Patience said, filling in the blank.

"Exactly! The End of Days, sister!"

They looked from one to the other thoughtfully.

"The Devil looks after his own," Melody said knowingly. The other two nodded and they all went back to work.

Clearly Creed had primed them for whatever I might say.

"Creed Kurgan *is* the Devil!" I shouted, starting to come unglued. "And the High Master . . . he sent another messenger cuz I was taking too long! *Him*" – I turned and pointed – "he's the messenger of the true High Master, the true . . . *Messiah*! He came to bring you to safety. We must free him! Really, we must—"

"Really? We must?" Melody said, uncharacteristically ticked. "What we really *must* do is get you ready. Father is waiting!"

They stood me up and began draping me in colorful layers of silk fabric.

"OK. OK. Listen. OK. He's not a messenger."

"We know that," they said in unison.

"He's a cop!"

They gave me a "tell us something we don't know" smirk.

"OK. He's a cop. But do you know why he's here?"

They had an answer, but they wouldn't give. Creed had surely given them some b.s. about Skinner being an agent of a corrupted government of unbelievers who were plotting against them.

"Well, *I'll* tell you the truth. Without the b.s.! That man over there – that cop – he's my friend and he came to Pie Town cuz I've been charged with killing Rabbit Rawlings! And he knows I didn't do it! And that man over there, he's got a wife and two little girls, too. And they were all drugged and kidnapped and brought here! And you know where they are! And you have to tell me, now! *Where are they?!*"

They exchanged looks again and smirked. They weren't buying it. I struggled to get away from them.

"*Please*, hold still," Daisy pleaded. "If you keep wiggling—"

My knees buckled. Daisy grabbed me under the arms, pressing into an open cut.

"Stop! You're hurting me!" I howled.

"Stop hurting her," Skinner yelled, yowling in agony as he struggled futilely to come to my aid.

"Uncuff his legs! Uncuff his hands! His blood can't circulate! He'll die if you don't!"

They ignored my pleas. I started to cry.

"*Please*, Melody." Bupkis. "*Please*, Patience." Bupkis. "Daisy, he killed your boyfriend! *Please*—" Bupkis.

I tried one last time to get free from their grip, but I was too weak and I couldn't tolerate the pain that shot through my body with each movement.

"At least loosen his binding, just a little bit," I fell to my knees and begged. "*Please.*"

"Now, don't resist us, Honey."

"We're only here to bring you to the New Light."

"Let us clean your retribution rewards."

"*Retribution rewards*?" I snickered. "Yeah, I guess I earned just about enough *retribution rewards* to get myself damned near beaten to death! What about you gals? You stupid, balloon-headed retards! You belong to the same frequent flyer program as I do, you know! And you're racking up reward points by the second! Which one of you lucky gals is gonna be next to collect?"

I tried to rip the fabric from my body, and yelped when I got hold of a piece of gauze instead and yanked off a scab.

"Honey, let them take care of you," Skinner said. "Save your strength."

I turned to see if he was looking at me. He wasn't. His eyes were closed but his mouth was moving. *Was he praying?*

"OK, pardner," I whispered, wearily.

They tended to the exposed wound, then got me back on my feet and finished covering me in fabric. I stared at my face while they worked. It looked like it had been flattened by a hot waffle iron – a combination of little boxes and, where it was healing, little crosses – little crucifixes. *Jesus died for somebody's sins, but not mine.*

When they finished my body, they tore the fabric in strips and wrapped them around my ankles and feet, leaving my toes exposed. They were as happy as if they had good sense. They told me they loved me. They told me they would fight to the death to protect me. They told me that I would soon be the mother of a new world order. They warned me about the Devil and told me not to be like the fool who is thirsty in the midst of water. They said they forgave me for the bad names I'd called them. 'It's the Devil fighting for your soul,' they said. But he wouldn't win, they said, cuz *The Gift*, the *New Light*, the *Prophet*, their *Father*, their *God*, had chosen *me* to birth the Fourth Wave and that I was *the* luckiest woman in the whole world. "Small world," I said, and waited half-heartedly for a laugh. None came.

We walked slowly out of the cell. Melody and Patience and Daisy coaxed me gently forward with encouraging words. We moved down the damp corridor, past the stockroom, the post office, and through the room with the printing press. I noticed a stack of newsletters, bound, ready for distribution: *The Fourth Wave* – latest edition. I wondered briefly if Alice had seen the last one. *Had she noticed anything funny about the population of Pie Town? Like the X through the number 86, and the hastily scribbled number 87 above it? Or maybe those zigzag lines that looked oddly like lightning bolts?*

They helped me climb the creaking stairs and finally we entered the living room. The walls were lined with beautiful shiny fabrics in primary colors, and little lights twinkled around the borders of the large picture windows. Something tickled my toes. Feathers. I was walking on feathers: I was ankle-deep in little white feathers. Suddenly the room lit up as the lightning put on a show in the distant fields. It was quite a sight. If only things had been different. If only, if only. A million if onlys.

The guests – the *amplitude* – were seated on the floor amid the feathers – men on one side, women on the other. They were totally ripped – a bunch of sexed-up psychedelic kill-crazy brain-dead nitheads – eyes glazed over and faces plastered with the Joker's super-sized grin – stretching from ear to ear. My body shook involuntarily. It wanted drugs. Real bad. I felt disturbed and disoriented. But I had to stay straight. I had to concentrate. Skinner needed me.

The Droid Sisters walked me up the aisle to the altar – a long rectangular table covered with flowers and bowls and vials of liquid and . . . instruments . . . sharp-looking instruments. Suddenly Minister E. Benezer Stryker entered the room, wearing an outrageously ornate red and gold ceremonial outfit. When he stood in front of me I got a case of the giggles, and he told me to cut the comedy. Then Big Tiny entered. She was wearing skin-tight red leather pants and a matching studded leather jacket that hid her tiny tits. She stood next to Stryker. I looked at Big Tiny. She gave me a wink. I looked at the instruments on the table. *Aha,* I thought. *I'm not losing a clitoris tonight, I'm gaining another hand-poked Tebori tattoo. Phew.*

A loud gong sounded. Everyone turned, and the back door opened and everyone stood. When Creed crossed the threshold, you could hear a pin drop. He strode confidently up the aisle, his eyes burning with determination. He stood beside me at the altar.

"Real gods require blood," he whispered into my ear.

He was a fucking nut job. So was everyone else in the room. And what about me, the gal who just wanted a little normal, a little attention? What the fuck was *I* doing in this loony bin?

■　■　■

Right now a small child is delighting as red sticky watermelon juice drips down the sides of her mouth and makes a mess of her new Sunday dress. Right now a baby is entering a world where it will have to carry its own weight. Right now a little girl is discovering that raisins taste better when they go from the box to her fingernail and then into her mouth. Right now a puppy is so excited to see its master that it's peeing all over the floor. Right now a single mother is worried that she can't care for her child any longer. Right now someone is feeling sorry for herself, while somewhere half-way around the world two lovers are about to kiss for the first time, and when they do – when their lips touch – the earth will open and swallow them whole. Right now someone is crossing a line and can never turn back. And right now, in a place somewhere outside of Pie Town, a gal named Honey McGuinness is about to exchange holy vows with a man named Creed Kurgan. Somewhere something is always happening.

■　■　■

I looked into his eyes. He was hungry, and not just for another side dish. He was ready for the whole fucking enchilada. We faced each other. Stryker motioned with both hands. Creed bent down and laid two beautiful pillows at our feet. He knelt on one, then reached up and took hold of my hands and gently pulled me down onto the other. We knelt, face-to-face. The sound of ringing bells slowly filled the room, and feathers floated down from above, and the twinkling lights turned from white to red to pink. For a coldblooded serial killing maniac, this fella sure did know how to throw a party.

"Today," Creed began, as the bells died down, "you, Honey McGuinness, shall join me in a new Garden of Eden."

He stared into my eyes. I leaned forward slightly and whispered into his ear, "I wish I was dead." He whispered back, "Dying is easy. Living is the hard part."

Didn't I know it.

"We are about to enter the Fourth Wave," he bellowed, turning from me to look at the amplitude. "I am your Father. What do you have to say?"

One by one the Bobby Beausoleil wannabes stood and declared themselves to be homosexuals and pedophiles, then kissed Creed's feet.

"I am your Father, your Lover, your God. What do you have to say?"

One by one the Leslie Van Houten wannabes stood and denounced themselves as whores. They named and condemned their past lovers – saying each was impotent and unable to please her. Then they started to gyrate and whipped themselves into a wild frenzy, shouting, "We love you Father."

"Sit, my amplitude! Be my witnesses!" Creed said, then nodded to the minister.

"We gather here tonight to join together Creed Kurgan and Honey McGuinness in holy matrimony. Join hands. Repeat after me: I, Honey McGuinness, do take Creed Kurgan for my lawfully wedded husband, to love and honor until death do us part."

I tried, but the words wouldn't come out. Stryker took me through them one at a time.

"Repeat after me: I, Creed Kurgan, do take Honey McGuinness . . ."

Big Tiny handed the rings to Creed. He slipped mine onto my stub. And just like that, *kowabunga*, it was official: I'd been given away.

"Big Tiny couldn't find any unblemished area of flesh for your tattoo. Don't be disappointed. As soon as you heal you'll have it. In the meantime, I've got a surprise for you."

My "wedding dress" was scrunched and rumpled – half on, half off. I was being led down the stairs towards the cell.

"What happened last night, after— " I asked groggily.

"We celebrated. You were the life of the party once Dr. Cocker relieved your . . . *discomfort* . . . with a generous mixture of morphine and camphonated tincture of opium. The amplitude partied till dawn. We, of course, went to bed early," he chuckled.

I looked at my disheveled clothing.

"Did we—"

"Consummate our union? All night long, baby!"

He laughed insanely and pulled me down the dark hallway to the cell. I looked through the iron bars. There he was, Skinner, squirming and groaning in the corner.

"Please, let him go," I said softly.

Creed ignored me and signaled for Hurricane. Hurricane opened the cell door, undid the ropes that had Skinner's legs trussed like a calf, and hoisted Skinner into a sitting position. Skinner, hands still cuffed, yowled in pain. Creed shoved me. I fell down near Skinner. Creed looked back and forth behind us several times – his eyes burning and focused as a laser beam.

"Life and death by irony!" he roared, spreading his arms wide and throwing his head back.

Life and death by irony? What the fuck did that *mean?* I looked at Skinner. He looked at me and shook his head slightly. Creed snorted and took a step forward.

"Welcome home, son of a bitch."

Skinner squinted.

"Mind your manners, boy," he smiled ominously. "Say something polite to your step-mother."

Skinner looked at me. My heart stopped.

"What? What are you saying?" I asked.

He ignored me and signaled to Hurricane. The bum-fuck picked up the broken eyeglasses and put them on Skinner's face. Creed stepped closer.

"Do I know you, sir?" Skinner asked, straining to see his face.

"'Familiarity breeds contempt,'" Creed said, taking another step closer.

Skinner tilted his head.

"My pa always said familiarity breeds *understanding*."

Creed bent down so's they were eye-to-eye.

"Is that what your pa always said?"

Skinner tilted his head in the other direction. His mouth fell open slightly. I could hear his breathing, erratic and heavy.

After an unbearable silence, he whispered, "*Pa?*"

Creed stood and booted Skinner in the side. He slumped forward with a grunt.

"Don't call me that, you son of a bitch!"

"*But . . . but . . . I thought—*" Skinner wheezed.

"Shut your mouth and listen!" He kicked him again, then started to pace. "Your mother was a whore and you are her bastard son! She told me all about it. Yes, she did. She said it was just a *mistake*. She said she was *sorry*. She begged me to forgive her." He snorted. "She said he meant nothing to her – he was just some traveling salesman!" He scoffed. "She said it only happened once! Once!" he hollered, his voice rising louder with each word. "Like that made it OK! OK, that she opened her whoring cunt to some fly-by-night hard-on and spawned the Devil's child in sin so great that it destroyed her womb forever! Destroyed her womb forever! Denied me my rightful progeny!" He stopped pacing and stood in front of Skinner and lowered his voice. "I told her I forgave her," he smiled wickedly, "but I never forgave her. She had to pay for her sin. She had to burn in Hell for what she did."

He waited for this information to sink in. Eventually, it did.

"*You? You started the fire?*"

"You were at school. She was making pancakes. I carried my boots to the table and set them down. She served me. I drank some coffee and ate.

I lit a cigarette. Then I got up and came up behind her. I put a plastic bag over her head. Oh, Jezebel."

He paused and paced, and we waited in stunned silence. Then he abruptly stopped pacing and bent down just inches from Skinner's face.

"Cursed is a shameless bitch," he said pitilessly. "I doused the house with gasoline. I watched it burn to the ground – ash and smoke. I made my way to the road – just the clothes on my back – and hitched a ride on a semi heading east." He snickered. "A fire truck sped past us in the opposite direction about twenty miles down the highway, sirens blaring. 'Probably a cat stuck up a tree,' the long-hauler said, and we both laughed like crazy." Creed stood and started to pace again. "Of course, no one ever suspected a thing. Small-town tragedy. Read all about it. Poor Bill Ochs and his wife – burnt beyond recognition. Poor Skinner Ochs, orphaned. They found a few unidentifiable bones – charred – and two tin coffee mugs and what might've been a pair of boots." He laughed maniacally. "They were right! Bill Ochs did die that day! And Creed Kurgan was born!"

"I don't believe you, you're— "

Creed gave him a whack to the side of his head.

Gasping for breath Skinner asked, "Where's Mary? Where are my girls?"

"Mary?" Creed asked, like he didn't know.

"Mary. My wife, Pa."

Creed punched him. "I told you, don't call me that! And as for Mary . . . well, Mary's been a little lamb."

Creed snickered and looked at me. Skinner followed his lead.

"What?" Skinner groaned softly. "What about Mary?"

"Yes, Honey. Tell your boyfriend about our little lamb."

"He's not my boyfriend, you fucking psycho!" I screamed.

"My wife is disrespectful," Creed said to Skinner. "She defies. She lies."

Skinner tried to say something, but Creed put his finger to his mouth. "Shhh. Shhh." Then he turned and walked towards me.

"The transgression of the Fallen Goddess is at work! You are the work of the Devil."

"*You* are the work of the Devil!" I yelled.

"Ah," Creed sneered. "And so she opens the Gates of Wrath."

He ripped what was left of the fabric from my body. I shrieked in pain and bit him hard. He smashed me in the yap. Skinner shouted and struggled in vain against his restraints. Creed told Hurricane to hold me down.

I told Hurricane his mama would be ashamed of him. Creed punched me again. Fresh blood poured from my re-opened wounds.

While he raped me he told me not to be frightened. He said the Devil had taken possession of my body long ago and had used me to seduce Skinner, to turn him into an adulterer, just like his whore mother. He said Satan, in an act of irony and arrogance, had manipulated the forces of nature to bring his bastard son to him now, in an effort to defeat Creed Kurgan. It was now a battle for domination, a battle for World Order. But Creed Kurgan would never surrender. The Devil was clever indeed, but not as clever as him. It would take time, he said, and it would be painful, but Creed Kurgan would triumph. The Forces of Evil would be exorcised from my body and I would be re-formed and purified. I would be the Mother of the children of Creed Kurgan. I would give birth to the Fourth Wave. Nothing could or would stop him.

"Oh, my Honey girl," he said, pumping into me savagely, "you've been used and abused. But now you are my wife, Mrs. Creed Kurgan! Hold fast against our enemies!" He growled and fucked me faster. "Oh, yes. Redemption is near. I can feel it," he said, ruthlessly ramming into me. "Can you feel it, baby? Oh, yeah, *here it comes! Get ready! Oh, Holy Mother Mary! Oh, Holy Brother Jesus Christ! Creed Kurgan your Savior cometh!*"

■ ■ ■

In my dream my family is edible. My mother is a Fig Newton. My father is the Pillsbury Dough Boy. And I am a loaf of bread.

"I didn't know. I didn't know he was your . . . father."

Was it possible for a gal to wake up crying? It was.

"Is he? I don't know. How could you know? He was dead. I thought he was dead."

I covered my body with the blanket and dragged myself across the dirt floor – uttering a series of painful ouchs and eeks – and slumped next to Skinner. His mouth was covered in dried blood, just like mine. I gently removed his shattered glasses, and stared into his beautiful blue eyes. They were filled with questions. *Why? How?* We both choked up.

"Oh, God. This is a nightmare," I whimpered, shivering from cold and horror.

"Come closer to me, pardner," he said tenderly. "You'll warm up."

I inched closer till our bodies were touching, and let myself be unruffled by his heat.

"I didn't know," he said. "All these years . . . I thought . . . I mean, he says he's not even my real father."

"Oh God. I'm so sorry, Skinner. I'm sorry I got you into this. I shouldn't have called—"

"Mary told me you called. She told me you said 'Home is where you *live*, not where you love' – and that was wrong. You got it backwards. I wanted to call you to tell you what my pa had always told me." He choked back tears, then pressed on. "'Home is where you *love*, not where you live.' *That's* the way it goes. I wanted to tell you so you wouldn't be misled. Mary said you were living in a town named after a dessert." Tears rolled down his cheeks. "She couldn't remember the name. She said you didn't give her a phone number. Said you were leaving town with some guy."

"There never was a fella back then. I was just pretending cuz ... Oh God, I wish I'd never made that call! Forgive me, Skinner. Please. I didn't know ..." I shook my head back and forth and the tears burned into my open wounds.

"No regrets between us, Honey. I'm glad you called. I'm glad they traced the call to me. You were in trouble."

"I didn't kill anybody. I swear. *He* did it! Him and his Squeaky Fromme wannabes."

"He used to be ... he was a God-fearing man, a good man. He was a good father. If it's true ... what he says ... about being deceived ... about me ... about not being able to have kids of his own ... I don't know. Every man has his breaking point. He must've snapped. Gone off the deep end." He hung his head. "Whether he's my biological father or not, he's right about one thing: Bill Ochs died in that fire. And my ma ..."

He sobbed like a little boy. I wanted to comfort him but I couldn't. I felt so ugly and pathetic. "I'm awful sorry," was the best I could muster, while he struggled to regain some bit of composure – wiping his cheek dry on his shoulder and snuffling a couple of times.

"Tell me something, pardner," he said gently. "You met him when you were ... lonely ... OK, I get that. But why did you stay with him? I mean, you had to have seen how sick and dangerous he was."

"Things just got all balled up real fast," I shook my head. "I don't know. At first he seemed, well—" *Like he was just a great fuck? A great fuck that turned into a fucking nightmare so bad it was just a whole lot easier for me to drink the Kool-Aid than to try to get out?* "I don't know. Seems like I always miss the obvious."

We sat in silence for a minute.

"Tell me something else. He thinks I'm your boyfriend. Why?"

My face flushed at the thought.

"I never told him that. I never even mentioned your name. I guess he just made that assumption cuz you came to Pie Town and he heard we knew each other and he thought maybe you cared about me ... "

"I do care about you."

We each tried to adjust our bodies to find a less painful position, but neither of us could find one. We both moaned and then sighed in resignation.

"Tell me something else, pardner. The truth. What did he mean about Mary being a little lamb?"

I couldn't tell him what I suspected: Mary wasn't a little lamb, she was a lab rat.

"Who knows what he means? He talks such ... such ... *arkymalarky*."

He looked at me quizzically with a barely perceptible grin. My heart soared. *I made him grin!* It wasn't much, but under the circumstances ...

"Arkymalarky, huh?"

I nodded. He nodded. We both smiled sadly.

"So . . .Vlad the Impaler?" he asked, looking at me. "I mean, Genghis Khan, OK. Attila the Hun, I'm with you. But Vlad the Impaler?"

We both smiled sadly.

"You really married my ... this Creed Kurgan?" he asked, after a while.

I showed him my ring. He frowned.

"What happened to your finger?"

"I hacked if off cuz I couldn't stop counting up fives."

"Very funny."

I shrugged. We sat in silence for another couple of minutes. Then Skinner said, "And all this because you ran out of gas."

I thought about saying that it wasn't about running out of gas so much as it was about needing to get fucked, but I decided that that – and just about everything else I'd done since I met the man in the long coat – was best left unsaid.

"Honey. I'm sorry about ... I couldn't help you. I'm sorry I couldn't stop him from ... hurting you."

I put my hand to his mouth.

"No regrets between us, Skinner," I said. "Now, let me see if I can loosen your ankle cuffs."

"I wouldn't do that, if I were you."

We looked up. Creed was standing outside the cell holding a metal bowl.

"I was just—" I started.

"Silence!" he shouted. "Don't speak! Don't speak!" He began pacing back and forth, making animal sounds. He muttered something about Satan, then he threw the bowl through the bars. When it hit the ground a thick gooey glop of cum splattered onto my face. "Eat, pig!"

He took hold of the bars and fell to his knees. "I want to hold you," he said, morphing from Mr. Hyde to Dr. Jekyll. "I want to take away your pain. You are Daddy's girl. Daddy's good girl. You are Daddy's wife."

He stood and paced, rapidly. Hyde was back. "Oh, our secret sins are cast in the light of thy countenance! You whore! You cocksucker! Behold, I was shapen in wickedness: and in sin hath my mother conceived me! The wages of sin is death!" He started to rock from side to side. "And some people will seek death but not find it; they will long to die, but death will fly from them!" He stopped and grabbed hold of the bars again, pressing his face against the iron. Tears streamed down his face. "How beautiful are thy feet, O prince's daughter! The joints of thy thighs are like jewels, the work of the hands of a cunning workman. Thy navel is like a round goblet, which wanteth not liquor; thy belly is like an heap of wheat set about with lilies! Come to me, Honey. Come sit in the dust, O virgin daughter of Babylon, sit on the ground; there is no throne, for thou shalt no more be called tender and delicate! I have refined you . . . but not with silver." He sank to his knees. "I have chosen you in the furnace of affliction!"

"'God be merciful to a sinner,'" Skinner said calmly.

Creed looked at Skinner curiously.

"Your mother was a whore. She deserved to die."

"'Where mercy, love, and pity dwell, there God is dwelling too.'"

"'The father shall be divided against his son; and the son against his father.'"

Creed stood and put his hand on his johnson.

"No. No. No. No. No!" I cried.

"Your mother was a cocksucker. Not as good as your step-mother, though." He threw his head back and started to massage his bozack. "Watch and pray, that ye enter not into temptation; the spirit indeed is willing, but the flesh is weak."

He unzipped his pants and pulled out his hard pecker. I gasped and covered my face.

"Come here, wife. Show your boy what a good cocksucker you are."

"Stop it!" Skinner shouted.

"Keep your voice down, boy. You'll wake up the girls."

Skinner's face contorted. Creed sneered.

"You will mind your manners, or I'll have those two little girls brought down here. It's never too early to teach our girls how to perform their wifely duties."

"OK, Daddy," I said, fighting back tears. "That's it. We have to stop." I wiped the cum off my face and started to crawl towards him. "We have to go back to the way things were before. We can . . ." I could no longer fight the tears ". . . go back . . . please."

"Come suck me."

"Don't do it," Skinner shouted.

"Bring the girls," Creed shouted down the hall.

In a moment we heard their voices – their sweet innocent voices – calling for their papa.

"They're only a few steps down the hall. Shall I have them brought to us? What do you say, Papa? One at a time, or both together?"

"Stop!" I cried.

"You choose, boy," he said coldly. "I can do them one at a time or both together. I'm capable of feats greater than that! Your call."

Skinner hung his head.

"I'll do it! I wanna do it! You don't need them! *I'm* your wife! It's *my* duty! Let *me* do it!"

I crawled to the bars and got up on my knees. Creed smiled and shouted for the girls to be taken back upstairs. He moved forward, sticking his throbbing flesh through the bars into my open and waiting mouth. He reached through the bars and took hold of my head.

"Now do a good job. I wouldn't want to have to push your face against these bars. It might open some of your *retribution rewards*."

He held my head still and started to move in and out of my mouth.

"Oh, yes, that's right. That's my good girl. Oh, how I've missed your cocksucking mouth. Suck me good. Suck harder. Take me deeper."

I did like I was told.

"Oh, yeah. Oh, my sweet cocksucker. Daddy's going to give you his sacrament. Daddy's going to do just what you asked him to do – go back to how it was before. Sucking and fucking – all day, all night. Yeah, suck it good. You want it, don't you? Oh, yeah. Just like before. You want my fuck, don't you? Don't you? *I didn't hear you*."

I made a garbled sound, which was the best I could do with a mouthful of cock.

"Yes, of course you do," he laughed. "And . . . here comes Daddy's fuck."

He pressed my face against the iron bars and drove into my mouth.

"Swallow it! Every precious drop!"

I did like I was told. He let go of my head and slowly pulled himself out of my mouth. He stood back, breathing deeply through his nose and exhaling through his mouth. He zipped his pants.

"Now, go to your adulterous boyfriend, your stepson—"

"He's not my boyfriend! He was never my boyfriend. We never . . . he never . . . I swear!"

"Shut up! Satan doesn't speak the truth! Go. See if you have aroused the bastard."

"*Please*," I begged.

"Do it now, or I'll bring the girls to do it."

I looked at Skinner. His eyes were closed and his mouth was moving: he was praying. I looked back at Creed.

"I can't. No. I can't."

"You will. Yes. You will."

I crawled over to Skinner and did like I was told.

"Is he hard?"

"No," I lied.

Creed laughed mockingly. "Faggot!" Then he sighed heavily and walked away.

I moved quietly to the ratty blanket and wrapped myself up tight. Skinner didn't look at me. It was OK. There was nothing to say or do. I didn't plan for things to work out this way. And I didn't want it to be true, but it was: there was a part of me that wanted to know – just like Creed wanted to know. And when I felt Skinner's hardness, well . . . I knew I'd done a bad thing, an unconscionable thing . . . but I liked that he was hard, and I liked knowing that I was the gal who made him hard. I hated myself again, but this time, well, it felt kinda good . . . in a really sick fucked-up way.

"I've got something for you, faggot."

Two of the Prophet's bum-fucks dragged her body into the cell and dropped it in the corner. She was unconscious.

"Mary! Mary! What have you done to her, you sick . . ." Skinner struggled against the cuffs, and some modicker gave him a boot to the gut.

The only chance I had to save Skinner and his family was to convince Creed I was back on his side. Resisting, fighting, was a dead end.

"What have you done to the faggot's wife?" I asked casually.

Skinner looked at me, stunned and confused.

"We did what we had to do, my wife! She has sacrificed for *your* sake. The experiment went well. A few . . . hiccups . . . which is to be expected. But don't worry! *Your* modification will be flawless. You will be your husband's virgin. You will serve your husband's pleasure. You will birth his descendants from your virgin womb!"

My worst fears about Mary were no longer speculation.

"Yes. Yes, I will," I said eagerly, trying desperately to hide my hatred and disgust.

Skinner struggled to get up, rolling from side to side. Creed stepped forward and kicked him in the head. Skinner groaned. Creed looked at me, testing my reaction. I smiled sweetly.

"I am leaving her to you, Mrs. Kurgan." He signaled for Kasabian and Krenwinkel to bring in a box of first-aid items, towels, and a bucket of water. "But first, let me take a look at you."

I struggled to my feet and hung my head. I dropped the blanket. Creed growled. I tried not to, but I started to cry.

"Turn around."

I did like I was told.

He circled me slowly. His piercing gaze, his hot heavy breath inflamed my wounds. It felt as if he were beating me anew. I was overcome with dread. I couldn't bear it. I fell to my knees and clasped his legs and cried and begged. "Kill me. Kill me now, my husband. I am the whore. I am the sinner. Kill me, please. Anything. Just don't make these innocent people pay for my sins. Please." I looked up, boldly meeting his gaze. "Please, kill me. Let them go. They don't belong here. Please! Look at me! I am your wife! I belong to you! Do with me what you will! But please, let them go!"

He patted my head and I sobbed, and I thought about how my life was worth nothing and how death would be a relief. But not Mary and Skinner Ochs, who now, cuz of me, lay unconscious, beaten and mutilated. No, their lives were worth something. They were good people. They were a family . . . with two sweet little girls. They couldn't die like dogs. And I thought about how I wished I knew God – not the God Creed Kurgan – but the God that Skinner Ochs knew – a good God – a merciful God – cuz I wanted to pray for help. But alls I could do was pray to the human who had all the power. "Have mercy on them, *please*," I begged.

Creed continued to pat my head gently, and then he began to weep. This was it. I had to convince him that I *was* Mrs. Creed Kurgan. That I would birth the fucking Fourth Wave. It was the only way. I had to take the next step, without hesitation, all the way to the end of the road.

I struggled to my feet and stood before him, wiping the tears from his face.

"Fuck me, Creed. Please, your wife is begging you."

He smiled cruelly, a light twinkling in his demon eyes.

"Take me to our bedroom. I want to feel you inside me."

He pushed me back gently.

"Against the wall."

"No, not here!" I shouted. "Alone! I want to be alone with you! Just the two of us! Like we used to be!"

He backed me up against the wall.

"No! Not here! *Please* . . ."

He ignored my pleas and fell to his knees. He buried his face in my pussy, inhaled and howled. He stood, unzipped his pants, pulled out his hard rod, and then masterfully entered me without causing the slightest pain to my wounds. He held my hips motionless against the cool damp wall and fucked me, talking in a foreign language – a language I'd never heard before.

Stay calm, gal, I told myself. *OK. You didn't get out of the cell – you didn't get* him *out of the cell – but maybe you can still gain his trust. Be flexible. There's more than one way to skin a cat.*

I tried to think, to figure out my next move. But I couldn't get Skinner off my mind. I mean, I knew he'd close his eyes – I knew he wouldn't watch. But still. Still the thought of him getting hot and hard, combined with Creed's masterful control of my love-bud, well, it started to have a disgraceful effect on my body. I prayed to the God I didn't know to make Skinner as unconscious as Mary, so's he wouldn't hear my shame. But before I could say *Amen*, it came: the Biggest O of my rotten little life. And before I could catch my breath, Creed said, "Let's multiply the amusement . . . for your bastard boyfriend . . . and . . . your guest!"

He fucked me doggy-style. Then he flipped me over and I rode the baloney pony. Then he mounted me, spreading my legs so's I thought I'd split in two. He took his time – fucking me hard, fast, gentle, slow. He circled and pumped in deep and shallow thrusts. Around about my seventh orgasm he shouted, "Time to cleanse the leper" and ejaculated. Then he collapsed on top of me – crushing me beneath the overwhelming weight of his madness. I whispered in his ear, begging him to take me to our bedroom. He didn't respond. Instead, he got up and said he was going to restore his vital juices and make the final arrangements for my purification.

I was ashamed of myself. I wanted to say something to Skinner, but I couldn't. I went over and knelt beside Mary and stroked her head. But after a while the silence was insufferable.

"I'm working on a plan."

I looked over at Skinner, and to my surprise he was looking back at me. He was looking right at me, and he looked angry. Maybe he'd seen it all. Maybe, while his own wife lay unconscious in the corner and while his little girls were held captive, he'd seen the man who he knew as his pa – the good, God-fearing man who he thought was dead – and the gal he thought was his "pardner" – maybe he'd seen them fucking like wild animals. He was a prisoner, a man in pain, bound and humiliated . . . and maybe he couldn't help but watch.

■ ■ ■

I'd come to believe that a human being could get used to anything, no matter what it was, no matter how much it hurt. A soul could get used to the exploitation and abuse of its flesh . . . its mind . . . its heart. A soul could get used to living without – without love, without a home. So many things a human being could get used to. In fact, I hadn't found anything I couldn't get used to. And after all, I guess that was the Big Surprise in Life: like it or not – understand it or not – want it or not – the will to survive exists somewhere beyond our puny intellectual grasp, and, well, it's just damn near impossible to defeat. *So, being here in this cell, in this situation – well, in a way, I guess I felt right at home. But it was different for Skinner P. Ochs. He was as far from home as a fella could get.*

■ ■ ■

"I'm working on a plan," I said again.

"You think he's going to fall for that act?!" he yelled angrily. "He's crazy but not stupid!"

Well, how do you like them apples? He thought it was an "act."

"Couldn't act my way out of a paper bag. Sorry."

"I'm sorry I yelled. I'm sorry . . . what he did to you. I . . . I couldn't do anything . . ." He strained against his bindings. "I'm sorry . . . I'm sorry . . . Mary . . ." his voice trailed off and he choked up.

His voice had changed from anger to emasculated agony. An explosive pang of love and sadness filled my heart. Love, cuz Skinner Ochs was a man – not a little boy in a grown-up body. He was ripe and mature. He believed he was invincible – an unshakable tower of strength. He believed he was champion and defender and protector of the underdog and the ones he loved. He was a red-blooded American hero with a heart of gold, and he believed he was the guy who would always make everything OK. Sad, cuz under the circumstances he was none of those things. I started to cry.

"What's he done to Mary? What was he talking about, sacrificing? Will she be all right? Can you help her, pardner? Can you— "

"She's probably just drugged," I interrupted. As a matter of fact, I could smell the toxic yellow scourge of Special-T on her breath – what little breath there was. "She's gonna be all right. I promise."

I turned my back so's Skinner couldn't see what I was gonna do. He continued asking questions and I kept promising, and I pulled Mary's dress up to her waist. Blood covered both of her legs – dried black blood. I was right: she had been the guinea pig for Doc Cocker's female circumcision. Her vagina was sewed shut. Mary Ochs, with the vagina of a saint, had been sacrificed for *me*. She had paid for *my* crimes. *Oh, God.* I swallowed the vomit that filled my mouth.

"What kind of drugs? Is she . . . Talk to me! Did he . . . *touch* her?"

Oh, God. Had he raped Mary before he had her mutilated? It was all too sickening. I pulled her dress down and lay next to her, behind her. I curled up and put my body close to hers and wrapped my arms around her. Her skin was smooth, her body soft and warm. I could feel her heart beating, slowly. *I wouldn't let her die. I couldn't.* I owed her that much. I owed her more. She was the only woman I'd ever known in my whole entire life who'd made me a home-cooked meal. And how had I repaid her humanity? With a lustful shameless longing for everything that she was and everything that she had.

Why Mary? Why Skinner? It was my fault. I had crossed the border and they followed. But I couldn't have known. I couldn't have known he was really Bill Ochs. I couldn't have known he was Skinner's father. I couldn't have known all this would happen. It was just a freak accident, that's all. Yeah. It had to be.

I whispered repeatedly into her ear softly so's Skinner couldn't hear. "I swear, I didn't know any of this would happen. I swear, I didn't know. Forgive me."

"Honey! Talk to me!"

"She's gonna be all right, Skinner." I choked back my tears. "She's breathing real good – real strong. They gave her something to sleep. It'll wear off soon. She's gonna be all right. She just needs to sleep."

I used water from the bucket to wipe away the blood; it didn't come off easily.

"What are you doing?" Skinner asked, wired with fear.

"I'm just putting a cool cloth on her head," I lied. "Please, don't worry. She's gonna be OK."

"Tell me what he meant about sacrificing. What kind of *experiment*? I can't stand this! Get these bindings off of me! Oh, Lord, what did he do to you, Mary? Where are our girls? I've got to get out of here! Honey, what was he talking about?" he shouted desperately.

"Look, pardner. We've gotta stay calm. We've gotta make a plan. We've gotta keep our voices down, be still, for Mary's sake. Let her rest. The drugs will wear off soon."

I checked her pulse: barely there. I breathed my breath into her mouth so's her heart would keep beating.

"Bring her over here to me, Honey. Bring my Mary to me."

I couldn't do that; he would see what they had done to her. I left Mary and went to his side. His head was bleeding.

"Let me take care of you."

"No! Forget about me! Bring her here!"

"She shouldn't be moved," I said gently. "Stay calm. Let's just let her rest."

I got the first aid kit and went to work on the gash in his left temple. He winced when the alcohol touched the raw flesh.

"Hold still. I said I've got a plan. I'll get us outta here." I covered the cut with a bandage. "Look, let's face it. There's no way we're gonna get you out of these cuffs. So, the only way out of here is through Creed . . . Bill . . . whatever. Trust me on this. You may have known him as your pa, but I know him as Creed Kurgan."

"I don't want to hear about how you *know* him."

"OK," I said gently. "We need to rest. Let's close our eyes for a bit and then we'll talk."

Skinner didn't argue. He dropped his head and sighed heavily. I laid my blanket on top of Mary and curled up behind her again, holding her to me. I could hear Skinner sobbing. When he stopped, I closed my eyes. Before I fell asleep I thought that soon the three of us would be traveling together in the same dream – dreaming each other's dream. But when it came time to wake up, only two of us opened our eyes. Mary was dead.

Chaos. Creed and a dozen drones were in the cell and Skinner was yelling and trying to get at Creed. And Creed was shouting at Skinner to shut the fuck up and all the others were speaking in fucking tongues. And when Skinner kept yelling Creed kicked him in the same spot on the side of his head repeatedly until he shut the fuck up.

I crawled to Creed and wrapped myself around his legs.

"Please, Daddy. Let me come home with you. Let Skinner and the girls go," I begged.

He dropped a pair of panties on the ground next to me.

"*Oh, thank you,*" I cried, "*Thank you, Daddy.*"

I crawled over to Mary. It wasn't easy getting the panties on her cold, dead body. But when I did I started to bawl uncontrollably. Now, with panties on, she looked just like any other gal. Now she looked like she had a fine clitoris, an unharmed vagina. Now, no one could tell the truth.

"Unbind him!" Creed shouted.

Someone did as he was told.

"You're so right, my beautiful wife! It's time for you to come home! Get dressed!"

I took the bright silks from Squeaky Fromme and covered my body.

Skinner howled in pain. The cuffs had cut deeply into his wrists and ankles, and his limbs started to flap around spastically for lack of circulation.

"It's time! Let's go! The Fourth Wave awaits the virgin womb!" Creed shouted ecstatically.

Oh, fuck.

Skinner looked at me.

"Come on, son of a bitch bastard," Creed said. "On your feet!"

Skinner didn't move. He looked towards Mary. Creed nodded, and his bootlickers tried to grab Skinner's arm, but he lunged forward. The others tried to stop him from reaching her, but they couldn't.

"Oh, God. No! Mary! Mary!" he screamed when she didn't respond to his tenderness. He turned and lunged clumsily towards Creed. *"You motherfucker! You psychopathic lowlife motherfucker! You killed her! You motherfucker! You lowlife punk! I'll kill you with my own hands, you sick yellow-bellied motherfucker!"*

I looked at Creed. His head was tilted down, his eyes looking straight from Skinner to me. He blinked slowly. A chill ran through my body. I knew exactly what he was thinking. *Th-th-th-that's all folks*, I thought. I'd never heard Skinner cuss, not once – no matter how tough a jam he was in. But now he'd gone and done it. He'd used *exactly* the right word . . . at *exactly* the wrong time.

"What did you say? What did I hear? *Motherfucker?* Is that what I heard?" Creed smiled ever so slightly and looked around. He shouted, "Everyone out!" and then locked the cell behind them. He laughed and told one of the bum-fucks to go get the girls.

"You crazy motherfucker!" Skinner yelled.

"Motherfucker," Creed repeated mockingly. "Yes, I do believe irony is the hygiene of the mind – and, perhaps, even the body!"

Skinner's girls started to cry. They were close by, but not within eyeshot. They called out for their mama; they called for their papa to help them. Skinner put one hand to his bleeding head and closed his eyes.

"Creed . . . please . . . they're just little girls . . . they're scared . . ."

"Women are so intuitive. Psychic, some people say." His eyes twinkled with brutality. "Your mother was like that," he said to Skinner. "Perceptive. She thought I'd never leave her. She thought I loved her too much. I guess she was right about that. But," he laughed, "she was wrong to think I'd forgive her!" He paced, then continued, his voice rising over the growing cries of the girls. "But she knew her sin could never be pardoned! Do you know how I know that? Because she didn't struggle. She let me put that plastic bag over her head. She let me take the life from her body. She knew it was her only hope of salvation! And because of that I promised her one thing . . . that I would never see her bastard boy again. And I would have kept my promise, but . . ." he shook his head and whooped. "But you came looking for me! *You* found *me!* You sorry son of a bitch. Your whore mother took everything from me. Everything! And while she burned in Hell, I fretted day and night about the state of *my* soul. But then, one day it happened – as simple as a sneeze! I got under *conviction*. I got Jesus! And then the truth of the ancient Kurgan Law was revealed to me, and I was reborn! I was God! I would lead the Final Wave! And when I turned that corner, it was just like a light from Heaven broke over my soul and the great burden of that whore just rolled off my heart and I was set free! Free to be me!"

The girls started to scream. Creed shouted for them to shut up. Skinner stared daggers at Creed. Creed's eyes rolled back in his head.

"A vision of the willful bitch came to me, having a hand full of abominations and the filthiness of her fornication, and upon her forehead was written a name, Mystery, Babylon the Great, The Mother of Harlots and Abominations of the Earth. Let no man deceive you with his words; for with these words cometh the wrath of Kurgan upon the child of disobedience. And you – yes, you – are about to experience the wrath of your own words. *You* are about to become the motherfucker!"

"No!" I screamed. "No! I belong to *you – only to you!*" I ripped the clothes off my body and stood up. "Look!" I said, pointing to my tattoo. "It's written on my body! *I belong to you!*"

Skinner's mouth opened slightly when he read the words on my belly. But then he seemed to gain his composure. He shouted in a calm but firm voice for his girls to quiet down.

"An enemy has Honey on his lips!" Creed said, and knelt down so's he was face-to-face with Skinner. "I know you have fucked her before, and—"

"That's not true!" I protested.

He raised his hand and continued, "And you will fuck her one last time, before she becomes my Vestal Virgin!" He stood and walked over to the cell door and took hold of the iron bars. "Now, you may look for some absolution based on some . . . *technicality* . . . but you won't find any. Why? Because you believe I am your father . . . and if I am your father and Honey is my wife . . . well, as a matter of fact, that will make you the only actual mother fucker in the room!" He laughed, and the automatons giggled. "Now, go ahead. Fuck your mother. We will witness your deliverance."

I objected, hysterically. Skinner simply said, "No."

"Would you have those girls be your witness? Would you have them see the dead body of the woman who was the origin of their sin?"

There was nothing to say. I was, at that moment, as cold and dead as Mary. I didn't care anymore. I had survived so much pain, neglect, agony, and humiliation in my unholy life that it didn't even matter what was about to happen next. But I didn't know if Skinner could survive – even for his girls. I looked at him. He was still, but not weak.

"Go, good girl. Whisper something enticing to your son. Something that will engorge his faggot pecker!"

I moved slowly towards Skinner and cupped his ear with the palm of my hand so's only he could hear my words. "I would give my life for Mary's. I am the one who deserves to die. Forgive me. Please forgive me. I'm going to kill him. I will. I don't care what happens to me. But you have to live – for Rosa and Ruthie."

He put his arms around me and I started to cry.

"Well, that's very touching ... but disappointing," Creed sneered. "I've ... I mean, *we've* never known our Honey to be lacking in lasciviousness or fancy – verbal or corporeal! But since she fails us, well, we'll just have to play Simon Says. Heed me well, or I'll have the girls fetched. Four can play this game just as well as two!" He snorted. "Now, Simon Says, 'Sit against the wall, bastard.'"

Creed unlocked the cell door just long enough to let Angel in. She was grinning from ear to ear like a bear in a berry patch – which was all she ever did and all she knew how to do. Her eyes were glassy, her pupils pinned. She was ripped out of her fucking gourd. *I could use some of that.*

"Take the blanket, Angel. Lay it in front of the bastard. Honey, go lay on your back. Open your legs, so the son of a bitch can see. Good. Now, Angel, do exactly as Simon has instructed you! You remember, don't you?"

Angel said she did, then she disrobed. She had a fleshy, voluptuous body. She was perfect. She had no deep gashes crisscrossing her flesh; her skin was pink and rosy. Her long red hair was shiny and clean, not dirty and matted with dried blood. She was beautiful. She was everything I was not.

Angel knelt between my legs and began to lick my girlfriend. Her tongue was gentle and, well, educated. *OK, maybe I'd judged Angel too harshly. Maybe she could do something other than grin.* She placed her body so's her behind was facing Skinner with her legs spread, giving him an unobstructed view of her head buried in my muff.

"Oh, yes. What a perfectly sinful performance," Creed rasped, foaming at the mouth.

Angel sat up and started to play with my yum-yum, pulling the lips apart and fucking me gently with her fingers. *Was Skinner watching?* I peeped quickly. *Yes.* She moved to my nipples, twisting them between her fingers and making them hard. Then she sucked them and licked my face, cleaning my wounds. Then she kissed me passionately, sticking her tongue down my throat. I tried real hard to feel bupkis.

"Honey, turn over and get on your hands and knees so that your ass is exposed to your son," Creed ordered.

I did like he told me and Angel came and straddled my back, facing Skinner. She wet her fingers and spread the cheeks of my bottom. She started to circle my anus with very skillful fingers. Then she wet her fingers again and spread the lips of my chucky. Then she dittled my hot spot. I didn't know if my stepson was watching or not. I tried to and succeeded in stopping myself from finding out. Angel put one finger in my asshole and one in my vagina and fucked me like that for a few minutes. Then she removed her fingers and bent over me and sucked and licked and ate out one hole and then the other. *Yep, that settled it. The gal definitely had other talents.* I made a little gasping sound, and quickly cleared my throat to cover it up.

"Angel is red on the head like the dick on a dog!" Creed shouted gleefully.

Re-energized by her prophet, Angel came behind me and gave it to me doggy-style using her fingers. At the same time she played with herself and made her nipples hard.

"Simon Says, 'Mother is ready!' Don't you move a muscle, my good girl!"

Angel dismounted and moved towards Skinner. I watched, but held still. Angel unzipped Skinner's pants, reached in, and pulled out his dick. He didn't resist, but he didn't exactly acquiesce either. He had full wood, but somehow remained defiantly unbowed.

■ ■ ■

Here it is. The moment of reckoning. But I'm in the wrong movie. It's not like I've pictured some plain ole meat and potatoes pop-a-chop. Fact, when it comes to Skinner P. Ochs, my sexual fantasies tend to be nasty, raunchy, sweaty . . . filled with wild excess. But that's just cuz I don't know better. And I don't know better cuz I don't know diddlysquat about diddlysquat . . . except one thing. Love hurts. But now it's about to happen, and well, seeing a very good man do a very bad thing isn't making me hot in the biscuit the way it's supposed to – the way it always does. Now that fancy is about to become reality, I can't stomach the perversion. So, I switch the channel to a G-rated movie. In it, me and Skinner are innocent and in love, happy and married, and alone in our perfect little bedroom in our perfect little house. Skinner has just come home from a long day on the beat. He's late, like usual. And, like usual, I've been worried. But I never really worry because I have Perfect Faith, and besides, I have to be strong for our perfect little girls – who are now sleeping soundly and safely in their perfect little bedroom across the hall after the three of us girls giggled our way through a dinner of mac and cheese and then splashed playfully in a bubble bath where I washed their perfect little-girl bodies and their sweet little-girl hair. He kisses me on the forehead and then takes a shower. I hear the water stop and my heart starts to race. He opens the door, and in the backlight of the bathroom I catch a glimpse of his naked body – so perfectly hard – so opposite mine – before he shuts off the light. He slips into bed and slides over to me, like he did last night, and the night before that, and every night for as long as I can remember. He wraps me in his strong, muscular arms, and I silently thank God because I am so perfectly blessed. Then he kisses me and I yield, perfectly. And we soar into the cosmos and nothing exists in the world except the two of us.

■ ■ ■

Creed instructed Skinner to sodomize me.

"Simon Says, 'Grab the back of her neck and hold her head down, hard. Press her face into the dirt. Fuck her good in her asshole, then fuck her good in her cunt.'"

I whispered, "Just pretend. Pretend this isn't happening."

Skinner said, "Never."

He followed what Simon said. Creed ordered him to say some dirty words, and Skinner complied. Then I did the same.

"What a good mother fucker! Ah, but I'm afraid, my children, that the bastard can't last – not like me! He will soon discharge, and all the fun will be over. Let me think. Yes. Simon Says, 'One more thrust, then pull out and turn her over. But don't worry. After a short break you'll find out what a good cocksucker your mother is!'"

Skinner did like Simon said, up to the turning me over part. But before he could take that "short break" or find out what a good cocksucker his mother was, he ejaculated . . . all over my body. I closed my eyes.

I knew Skinner was looking at me. I could feel his eyes burning right through my skin. But I couldn't open my eyes. I couldn't look at him. I was down for the count. But not Skinner. Even with cum dripping from his cock, even with his wife lying dead in the corner and his girls held hostage by a madman who might've been his father and who murdered his mother and was now forcing him to perform heinous sex acts on a disgusting piece of shit like me, and even though he knew that he would most likely be dead before the day was out, he stood his ground and faced the evil the way he faced everything in his face: with his eyes wide open. He was a warrior, and that heartbreaking fact started the waterworks.

"Bravo! Simon Says, 'You're done for now!'" He clapped his hands and unlocked the cell. "Bring the Uzis and let's roll! Salvation awaits!"

I opened my weeping eyes, confused. *What was happening?*

Skinner got up, zipped his pants, and then helped me to my feet. My bum leg buckled, and he steadied me. I avoided his eyes, and dressed as best I could.

A handful of Creed's brain-dead doped-up brownnosers arrived with the Uzis. They surrounded Skinner and marched him out. Creed came and extended his hand. I had no choice: I couldn't walk without help.

When we turned the corner of the hallway, Rosa and Ruthie ran towards their papa, grabbing his legs. Skinner looked a bit wobbly, but was strong enough to pick both girls up and hug them tight. *Skinner had his girls. Nothing else mattered.* Now, alls I had to do was figure out a way to distract Creed and his androids so that the Ochs family – what was left of it – could escape. Nothing else mattered.

The joint was jumping. They were all there – the whole whacked-out killer cult, including Cocker, Maggie, and a few faces I didn't know by name, but thought I might've seen around Pie Town one time or another. Some of the droids were armed and marching to orders. Some were staring into space and speaking in tongues. Some were reading aloud from a book titled *Kurgan Law*. And the rest were whirling out of control like fucking Sufi dervishes. The room was electric with psychedelic anticipation.

Creed grabbed my chin and turned my head. His eyes were ablaze. He raised his eyebrows and his lips curled. "Say, kids, what time is it?" he asked. With even a bird's turd of luck, "It's Howdy Doody time" would've been the answer. But when it came to luck, I was shit out of it.

Skinner sat in the corner, an Uzi pressed against his temple. Comforting clichés did little to calm Rosa and Ruthie when they were wrenched from his arms and taken away to the "big girls' room" by Daisy. I whispered "Daisy" as she passed. She gave me a sideways look. *Did she ever find the gun?* Her look told me only one thing: she was scared silly.

Creed directed the remaining bum-boys to sit and announced that they were about to witness the final purification of the Mother of the Fourth Kurgan Wave. They were about to witness Female Genital Cutting – a clitoridectomy, excision, and infibulation. He said the "FGC" would ensure submissiveness and modesty. He said the infibulation involved the narrowing of the vaginal opening through the creation of a covering seal. He said the vaginal opening would be sewn up and would only be unsewn – *opened up* – by Creed Kurgan. He said the fear of the pain of opening the vagina would prevent the Mother of the Fourth Kurgan Wave from participating in illicit intercourse, and the removal of body parts considered "male" would make her clean and beautiful. Stryker announced that it would then be through my virgin womb that their nation would be born.

"When pigs fly outta your ass, loaf head!" I jeered.

Creed told me to mind my manners. Then the doors opened and a large rectangular table was brought in – Big Tiny at one end, Maggie at the other. Big Tiny gave me a stoner's mindless wink-wink. I gave her and the red-head the hairy eyeball. Hurricane and Jet followed with a smaller table holding surgical instruments, bandages, and a tank of Special-T. They looked at me and beamed: they were higher than Mt. Everest.

Creed pushed me forward. My leg bowed. I lurched and fell. He grabbed my arms and started to drag me across the floor. I bit into his hand hard, drawing blood. Doc Cocker rushed to help him, but Creed stopped him by holding up his bleeding hand.

"The Devil desires blood!" he declared. "My blood. But he won't have my blood!" He socked me in the puss. I started to bleed. "He will have hers!"

Seeing my blood, the hopped-up bum-fucks started to fist-pump and cheer wildly. I struggled to get free. Creed tightened his grip. Then he bent down.

"You can make this hard, or you can make this easy," he said softly.

Was that true? Could I make it easy? I gave it some thought. *Maybe.*

"OK. I'll stop fighting. You can slice, dice, or puree me. I don't care. And I promise I won't make a fuss."

"Now, that's my good girl!"

"On one condition: let Skinner and the girls go."

Creed stood up and howled, "Mephisto wants to make a deal!" He kicked me in the side. "It is you, Dr. Faust, who has sold your soul to the Devil! It is you, Honey McGuinness, who has made a deal with the Devil! No! You can tell Mephisto, 'no deal'! Creed Kurgan will *never* make a deal with the Devil!"

He pulled me to my feet and kissed me passionately, forcing his tongue down my throat, then did the bump and grind. This drove the blue-balled droid boys into a frenzy of catcalls and whistles and applause.

I let myself be manhandled. I needed time to think. I scanned the room. Skinner was looking right at me. Even if I let them do the slice-and-dice, Skinner was a dead man. And, even if I survived, what were the odds that I could save the Ochs girls? Slim to none.

I looked at the front door. I looked at the back door. Could I make a run for it? Even if I could, what good would it do? I looked at the picture windows. I saw something move. *What was it?* I blinked and looked at Skinner. He followed my eyes.

Creed joined in the feverish frenzy of testosterone, then shouted over the crowd, "It's time to ring the doorbell! Pick the rosebud! Snip the clit!" and pushed me forward. "Let each of you be witness!" he shouted. "The destruction of the work of the Hystera is finally at hand! This is our only path to salvation! Do not fear, Mother! The instruments of your purification await! Your re-formation is at hand!"

And just when I thought my goose was cooked, I heard it. It was barely audible, but unquestionably . . . the *arf arf* of a dog. A mollycoddled mongrel about as big as a peanut. *Romeo.* On the third *arf* Alice tumbled through the front door. She was wearing some kind of uniform and carrying a small cardboard box – *my cardboard box!*

"Lordy, Lordy! We've been knocking for a coon's age," she said, looking down so's she wouldn't trip over the yapping mutt who charged into the room between her legs. "Oh, don't mind my little man," she said absently, then looked up. "We've got a delivery here . . ," she said, growing more tentative as she took in the scene, ". . . for Miss Honey Mc . . ." Her voice trailed off. She dropped the box and started to back up. "Well, don't bother about us. We'll just show ourselves out. C'mon, Romeo." But Romeo didn't c'mon. Instead he went over and started to jump up and down on Jet. Alice stopped. Her mouth dropped open. "*Clyde?*" she said to her twin with the indented temple. "*Clovis?*" she said to the one without the indent. Her eyes continued to search the room. "Father Stryker?" "Maggie?" "Is that Tommy Horton?" "Oh, Lordy, Lordy—"

Suddenly a voice boomed over a loudspeaker, announcing that the compound was surrounded by FBI and ATF agents and they had a search warrant to enter the premises and all occupants were to exit immediately, hands up. Before I could say Jackie Robinson, Creed ordered the bum-fucks to their defensive positions and told them to open fire. And after they did, the gates of Hell opened up.

A hail of gunfire rained into the room – from every side, shattering glass, taking down Doc Cocker and a couple of the amplitude boys. Suddenly a titanic tank plowed right through the front wall into the room, crushing everyone in its path. Then it pulled back and another vehicle pulled up, took aim, and launched several grenades into the room. They exploded before they hit the ground. Body parts flew through the air. An arm landed on the floor next to my feet . . . tattooed with the black W.A.V.E.S. design.

Creed laughed and put his hand under my clothes and tried to get a finger into my hoo-ha. *Not this time, buster.*

"Get off me, you fucking whack job!"

I swung around and gave him an elbow to the right side of his head with everything I had. Which may not have been much, but was enough to knock him to the floor. He landed hard on his back. A barrage of tear gas canisters, lobbed into the room from every direction, started to hiss. A fire started to blaze at the far end of the room.

"Don't go! Don't go! It's not over!" Creed yelled, reaching out and grabbing hold of my leg.

All of a sudden Romeo charged and latched onto Creed's hand – the hand that was still bleeding from where I'd bit him – and Alice's little man started to gnaw into his flesh ferociously. Creed yelled and swatted at him. Hurricane ran by and Romeo let go of Creed and charged after him, chomping down on his pant leg, and wouldn't let go, even though he was being dragged across the floor. Creed tried to grab me again, but I jumped back.

"Don't go! Don't go! We're so close!"

I looked down at him and laughed. Then I stepped on his hand. He squealed. I jumped up and down several times. He squealed more.

"All good things must come to an end, manhole!" I said, and squished harder.

The electricity was cut. The room went black, except for the sparks coming from the machine guns as the dumbfuck amplitude fired at the FBI and ATF. The whirl of a helicopter sounded above and something hit the roof and an explosion caused part of the roof to collapse, and sparked a new fire. I looked up and saw parachutes with illuminating flares and men dressed in black descending. The room was full of smoke and tear gas. It was getting difficult to breathe or to see. Then the *mano-a-mano* assault began.

Dunk Hayward lead the charge through the front door. FBI and ATF agents stormed in from the sides, the back, and above. All-out automatic weapons close-range combat ensued. Everyone was screaming. Bodies were dropping. The tear gas got thicker. I gave Creed a kick to the head, dropped to the floor, and started to crawl.

I slithered across the floor towards my box. I found it and ripped it open. I unwrapped the Raven and cocked it. Then I crawled through the thick stinging vapor towards where I'd last seen Skinner, bullets whizzing past my head. My eyes were burning; I couldn't see but a couple of inches in front of me. And then, a couple of inches in front of me, I ran into U.S. Marshal Duncan Hayward. He was covered in blood. I felt for a pulse. Bupkis. I moved on, crawling over one dead body after another. I heard Romeo. He was growling. I said "Good boy," and crept on. Then I heard Creed. I couldn't see him, but his voice was strong and clear. *Fuck.* "Man that is born of a woman is of few days, and full of trouble," he said. I crawled faster. Then I heard Skinner's voice. "No, Pa. Don't do it." I got up and ran blindly towards the voices through a volley of bullets. Then I heard Daisy cry, "Why did you kill him, Father?" Then Creed laughed and said, "Life's a bitch, and then . . ."

I lunged forward and pulled the trigger. The air lit up like the Fourth of July. I felt a sharp burning sensation in my belly and fell to my knees. Creed's body fell on top of me, knocking me backwards – the contents of his splattered brain leaking all over me. I pushed him off.

"... and then you die, motherfucker," I said, finishing his sentence.

Infection, dehydration, malnutrition, and a bullet that had to be removed from my belly kept me laid up in the hospital for more than a week.

When Skinner came to visit me he said the girls were doing OK. He said Daisy Clover told the FBI agents that she'd taken the Ochs girls and slipped out a side door before the melee started. She said she'd gone to one of the small bungalows, where she left the girls, retrieved a gun, went back to the main house, and shot Creed Kurgan one time in the head during the siege . . . cuz she thought he had killed her boyfriend, Rabbit Rawlings. When she was asked where she got the loaded handgun, she told them that she'd found it in a pomegranate tree. The agents asked if she was taking drugs. She answered "daily."

Since Daisy had confessed to shooting Creed, I didn't bother to mention my particular actions when the FBI agents came to question me in the days that followed. And since they didn't ask me about a loaded gun in a pome-granate tree, I figured Daisy never mentioned me, or, if she did, maybe they just chalked it up to drug-induced hallucinations. I didn't know whose bul-let killed the psycho, but I wasn't too worried. The gun Daisy used was big-ger and heavier than mine. I didn't think they'd perform an autopsy. Even if they did, and even if it turned out to be a .25 slug that killed Creed, they'd have to find the Raven and put it in my hands. And even if they did that, well, who was gonna argue that I didn't act in self-defense? Plus, I always had my fall-back defense: Stockholm Syndrome. According to FBI psycholo-gists, me and Daisy – two of the three cult members who survived the raid – suffered from a "paradoxical psychological phenomenon wherein the hos-tage expresses adulation and has positive feelings toward the captor." So's my only real concern was that they'd find my pistola and somehow connect it to two other unsolved murders. I liked my odds.

Skinner was in the room on the days the Feds came to question me. And it became clear that there were things he had neglected to mention to the agents too – like the fact that Creed Kurgan, aka Tommy Horton, was really Bill Ochs, and that – whether or not he was Skinner's biological father – he had confessed to the murder of Skinner's mother. I understood. Skinner was trying to cope and digest a whole new set of awful realities. I wasn't gonna do or say anything that would make matters worse. Skinner's mood was somber, his eyes teary, and his words sparse. Still, when the questioning got heavy-handed, he chipped in. He told the agents that I'd worked undercover with him to solve a homicide in the Big City, which was practically the truth. He hinted – although he couldn't say so "officially" – that I might still be working deep undercover, which wasn't even almost the truth. And he reminded them again and again that I'd saved the life of a fellow law enforcement officer, which was a matter of fact.

The bullet that was meant for Skinner had ripped into my lower belly. I'd taken one for my pardner, just like he'd done for me. I'd saved his life, just like he'd saved mine. He was alive cuz of me. And Rosa and Ruthie, well, they were alive too. That was the happy news. The sad news was . . . Mary. Poor, sweet, Mary: I didn't save her. Fact, she was dead cuz of me, her body incinerated with all the others in a raging out-of-control inferno.

Anyhow . . . Skinner was a cop and a cowboy and he spoke the lingo, and after the second day the Feds told me they didn't have any more questions.

■ ■ ■

The day before my discharge the nurse removed the bandage from my belly. When she was gone I got up and went to the bathroom. I looked in the mirror and laughed. The bullet wound was about the size of a plum – maybe a little bigger. It had obliterated the last word of my tattoo: CREED. Now it read: THIS PUSSY BELONGS TO. And I knew exactly what I would replace it with: a two-letter word that starts with "M" and ends with "E."

The newspapers were filled with stories about Creed Kurgan, World Advocacy for Values in an Enlightened Society, and the Fourth Wave.

It didn't take the swarm of reporters long to uncover most of the story. They reported that the Kurgans were what scholars called Indo-European or Aryan-language-speaking stock – a type that was in modern times to be idealized by Nietzsche and then Hitler as the only pure European race. The Kurgans were nomadic invaders who swept across prehistoric Europe, destroying physical and cultural Neolithic societies who worshipped the Goddess. The Kurgans were ruled by powerful priests and warriors, and they brought with them male gods of war. They gradually imposed their ideologies and ways of life on the lands and people they conquered. The one thing all the warring nomads had in common was a dominator model of social organization – a social system in which male dominance, male violence, and a generally hierarchical and authoritarian social structure was the norm. Another commonality was that, in contrast to societies that laid the foundations for Western civilization, the way the Kurgans and nomads characteristically acquired material wealth was not by developing technologies of production, but through even more effective technologies of destruction. It was reported that the Kurgan invaders had destroyed and conquered in waves. Kurgan Wave No. 1 occurred circa C. 4300-4200 BCE; Wave No. 2 circa 3400-3200 BCE, and Wave No. 3 circa.3000-2800 BCE.

According to newspaper accounts Honey Kurgan had become the "mother" of W.A.V.E.S, which, under the charismatic leadership of her new husband, Creed Kurgan, had been planning Wave No. 4 for over a decade. The plot was foiled in large part, the press reported, by one Alice Guthrie, owner of Alice's Motel in Pie Town. Mrs. Guthrie had deciphered a secret coded message sent to her by Mrs. Kurgan through the cult's newsletter, *The Fourth Wave.* "You see that? Right there in the corner?" Mrs. Guthrie asked reporters at a press conference, holding up the newsletter and pointing to the population count of Pie Town. "Well, that's Honey! See, she was always desperately wanting to be number 87 on the Pie Town welcome sign, but it just never did happen. So, when I saw that number written there, I just knew! I knew she was sending me a secret message, telling me she was still around these parts, and needing my help! And then right here," she said, pointing to three small marks next to the number 87, "well, those are lightning bolts! And I just knew! I knew she was letting me know she was near the Lightning Fields, 'cause everyone around here knows about the lightning fields. Honey sure did love to watch them." When asked about how she convinced local authorities to get involved and her participation in the raid she said, "I went to see Dunk, U.S. Marshal Duncan Hayward that is, bless his soul, and I told him everything. Now Dunk and I, we've been know-ing each other our whole lives, and Dunk knows I'm not what you would call a frivolous-type person. We took a drive out Quemado way . . . that's where the Lightning Fields are. The first day we didn't see anything, but Dunk had the idea to go back at night . . . look for lights. And don't you know, that's just what we did. And don't you know, that's when we found the compound in the woodlands, about five miles west of Quemado. Dunk said he had to call in the FBI; there were heavily armed guards at the gate. Plus he didn't know what he was dealing with, especially since Honey was wanted by the authorities on "unrelated" murder charges. A few days later Dunk came to me and said the FBI wanted to send in a civilian – to check out the situation – while they hid nearby. They wanted to defuse what could be a dangerous situation. I guess some folks get a lot nervous when they see FBI agents on their doorstep! Anyway, I came up with the idea of pretending to be a deliv-ery person, 'cause I just happened to have a personal box that belonged to Honey. The FBI agreed, long as I wore a bulletproof jacket. So, on the day of the raid, Dunk and some others took the guards by surprise and put their own men in their uniforms, and we drove through the gate and parked down the road a bit. Me and Romeo" – she patted her little dog's head and he kissed her on the mouth – "went to the door. We weren't supposed to go inside. We knocked and knocked and nobody came. We hollered, but no one could hear us; there were loud noises coming from inside. So, we decided to try the door and with a little push, well, we kind of fell into the room. And, 'cause we weren't supposed to go inside and we didn't come right out, well, I guess that's when the FBI . . ." she concluded with a vivid and horrifying description of the siege and the big, beefy federal agent who saved her life and to whom she was "forever indebted."

On a sad note, the accounts reported that Alice Guthrie's twin boys lost their lives in the raid – a raid that quickly stirred strong debate among government representatives and critics who called the FBI's use of deadly force a "gross over-reaction" that resulted in the "unwarranted and unjustifiable slaughter of innocent life." It was reported that federal agents used practices far outside the norm of standard operating procedures: the FBI and ATF used nine Bradley Fighting Vehicles and five M-60 combat engineering vehicles, which were obtained from the US Army; the ATF agents had their blood type written on their arms or necks – a procedure used by the military to facilitate speedy blood transfusions in case of injury. In addition, it was reported that agents approached the site in cattle trailers pulled by pickup trucks owned by individual ATF and FBI agents. Public outcry was growing, with calls for the resignation of the FBI Director and a full investigation by the Special Prosecutor.

In a separate story, the unrelated murder charges against Honey Kurgan, nee Honey McGuinness, were dropped after the full confession of E. Benezer Stryker, the only surviving "architect" of the cult. Stryker admitted his complicity in three murders: Officer Roberto Sanchez of the NMPD; Buddy Pinchback, cult member and Pie Town postal clerk; and the teenage cult-member-in-training and Pie Town resident Rabbit Rawlings. Stryker stated that Officer Sanchez had been murdered by Creed Kurgan and other cult members when they executed a sophisticated and successful plan to abduct the then-girlfriend of the cult leader from the Springerville Hospital, where she was recuperating from a finger injury and was in police custody for the murder of Mr. Rawlings. Stryker further stated that long-time Kurgan follower Buddy Pinchback was simply the victim of an unfortunate twist of fate that placed him in the wrong place at the wrong time. (Although the reporter pointed it out, Stryker didn't find any irony in his assessment of Punchclock's demise being attributed to "bad luck.") In the end, Stryker said, Buddy had to be killed in order to prevent him from regaining consciousness and pressing charges against the cult leader's wife-to-be.

The explanation of the Rabbit Rawlings murder took investigators into a further tangle of deception and intrigue. Stryker indicated to authorities that he had met Tommy Horton – who later changed his name to Creed Kurgan – a dozen years before, when he and his young bride, Maggie – another casualty of the FBI siege – had moved to Pie Town and bought the El Serape diner. The two men quickly found common ground and formed what Stryker called an "eternal bond" based on their mutual belief in male dominance and the dire threat to society caused by the "feminization of culture" and the "emasculation of masculine superiority." These beliefs, the minister stated, ultimately became a life's work after three formative and "miraculous" incidents occurred: Tommy Horton "discovered" the Kurgan Law; Tommy Horton was "slayed by our Savior Jesus Christ;" and Tommy Horton received the gift of prophesy from "our Savior the Lord Jesus Christ," at which time it was revealed to him that he, Creed Kurgan, Divine Father, would finally "correct the imbalance in the natural order of the universe." In order to provide "cover" for their "mission" and to ensure that they wouldn't "draw attention from law enforcement and other impotent unbelievers," a fictitious story was created and perpetuated by a submissive Maggie Horton – and one Joseph Cocker, M.D., a like-minded physician who practiced in nearby Springerville and who eventually worked exclusively for the cult. The fabrication went something like this… In a tragic accident, Tommy Horton fell down the stairs and had been paralyzed. Wheelchair-bound, the embittered, despairing, and rarely seen quadriplegic locked himself away in the couple's upstairs apartment and left the running of the business to his long-suffering wife. Thus protected, Tommy Horton was free to become Creed Kurgan and disappear for days at a time. He was also free to steal back and forth to the El Serape – usually in the middle of the night, hiding in the backseat of Stryker's vehicle. It was only when new recruits – after receiving years of indoctrination from Stryker at his ministry – finally took an oath to the cult and moved to the ranch that the dual identity of the "Prophet" was revealed, and then only to those who were old enough to remember and recognize Tommy Horton from before the fabricated accident. The ruse had worked well – funded through private donations and money that Maggie funneled and laundered through the El Serape – until one late night a few months back.

Rabbit Rawlings came back to church to collect some schoolbooks he'd left behind earlier in the evening. Hearing male voices, he stepped to the back. The door was ajar. Rabbit saw Stryker with a man he recognized as Tommy Horton walking around a car – a car that Stryker stated was to be sold to raise cash for the cause. Rabbit got confused: Tommy Horton couldn't walk; he couldn't even stand. When Stryker called the man "Prophet," the boy got scared. He dropped his books. The men looked at him. Then Rabbit ran. His fate was sealed on the spot.

What Stryker didn't report was that after Creed Kurgan met me and decided that I was "the one" and should become Mother-fucking-Hubbard to his deranged clan, he set me up for the murders . . . so's I wouldn't try to escape . . . so's I'd have nowhere to go . . . except Death Row. It wasn't too hard to figure what had happened to poor Rabbit. Stryker told him to get black spray paint and "detail" the stripes out of the Javelin: Creed didn't wanna take the risk of me seeing the car in town when Stryker put it on the market. Around the same time, someone who didn't like me much and wanted me out of town – which I guess wasn't so unreasonable, considering the rumpus I'd raised about the missing letters, which were probably stolen by Maggie cuz she was always going to folks' homes for supper, or some bum-boy android, or maybe even poor dead Punchclock, following Stryker's order – sprayed the message on the side of my trailer. I blamed Rabbit cuz Anita told me he bought the paint, and I went after him. When I caught up with him, he didn't know what I was talking about. That might've been that. But then the albino discovered Stryker and an ambulating Tommy Horton with the car he'd detailed, and then he discovered the Prophet's true identity. So, he got scared. He wanted to tell someone: me. He came to the trailer; I wasn't home. He tried to scratch off the unpleasant graffiti, gave up, and left me a note. While I was waiting for him to show behind the church, he was being murdered and stuffed into my closet. The events that followed and my overall condition at the time must've been like a wet dream for killer Kurgan, turning the frame-job into a piece of cake. *The luck of the Devil.*

In a story later in the week, the papers reported that in their search of the remains of the ranch, the FBI found an underground passage that led to two large "stone chambers." One contained an arsenal of automatic weaponry. The other contained thousands of religious artifacts stolen from Italy, Cyprus, Greece, and Peru. The artifacts included ancient tables, statues, and writing. In what appeared to be a systematic effort to eradicate any mention of the "Goddess" or the "serpent" that represented the Goddess in these priceless treasures – many of the items had been "altered" or "completely destroyed." Some relics, including documents penned by Catholic popes and a handwritten book preface by Italian dictator, Benito Mussolini, seemed out of place and appeared to be unaltered. In total, more than 3,000 artifacts – each meticulously documented in hundreds of large black notebooks, with an estimated value upward of ten million dollars, were found and would eventually be repatriated to the proper authorities in their countries of origin. The find would ultimately lead to the arrest of a network of plunderers and traffickers in black markets across several continents.

Most articles included the following statements: the cult leader, Creed Kurgan, had died of a single bullet to the head, fired by Daisy Clover; nearly one hundred cult members died during the FBI raid. Most casualties resulted from gunshot, fire, or suffocation by carbon monoxide inhalation. Only three cult members survived: Daisy Clover, Minister E. Benezer Stryker, and Honey Kurgan. Honey Kurgan had been shot once in the abdomen after surviving what appeared to be a vicious beating. After being kidnapped by the cult and taken to the compound, an out-of-state cop and his two daughters had survived the siege; tragically, his wife had not. Over two dozen law enforcement officials had been killed, including U.S. Marshal Duncan Hayward. Creed Kurgan's real name was Tommy Horton. Creed Kurgan, aka Tommy Horton, was a polygamist with two wives. There were indications that sex and sexual rituals, body mutilation, corporal punishment and imprisonment, and drug use were a regular and central part of everyday cult life; however, the three surviving cult members had so far refused to discuss these matters. *And, speaking as one of them, would continue to do so.*

Funnily enough, as it turned out, there were only two people on the face of the earth who could attest to what had happened in that cell between me and Skinner. One of them was a professional shapeshifter and secret-keeper: she would have no problem pretending the whole thing never happened. The other one, a deep-rooted and honest man, well, there was a good chance he lacked that particular talent.

I sat on the bench in front of the hospital thinking things over. When the Feds had brought me the key to my clunker I'd told them to give it to Lucky Frank. I'd taken his rifle and left his trailer a bloody mess; maybe it would square things up between us. That left me with one worldly possession, which was sitting in my lap: a sealed cardboard box. I was just thinking about how I had nowhere to go when suddenly I was swamped by reporters and camera crews, shoving microphones in my face and demanding answers to their questions. I started to cry. Someone reached through the crowd, took hold of my arm, and pulled me out: Skinner. He hollered at them to act civilized, but they didn't seem to know what that meant. He helped me into the front seat of his car. Ruthie and Rosa were asleep in the back. I tried to hide my ugly face as we drove towards Pie Town. It was a good forty-five-minute drive.

After maybe fifteen, twenty minutes of silence Skinner reached behind his seat and pulled out a brand new Donald Duck baseball cap and dropped it in my lap.

I smiled to myself and put it on, pulling the bill down low so's to cover myself as much as possible. I leaned my head against the window and looked out at the big blue sky and the unending wasteland.

"How did she die, Honey? The truth."

I knew the question was coming: I'd been dreading the moment. And I wanted to tell the truth, but I couldn't. See, I knew Skinner knew the truth: he had to. And I also knew that he couldn't handle hearing the words. So I said what any good pardner would.

"Drug overdose."

"That's the truth?"

"That's the truth."

He thought this over for a minute or two then said, "The rotten apple doesn't fall far from the tree."

I tilted my head.

"I left her to burn, just the way my pa left my ma," he explained.

"Hey, don't you do that to yourself!"

"Keep your voice down," he said, glancing quickly in the rearview mirror at his sleeping angels.

"You're wrong." I lowered my voice. "You didn't kill Mary. You didn't douse her in gasoline. You can't even compare . . ." I continued on, but I knew my words wouldn't make much difference. Cuz right then, fate, destiny, coincidence – whatever you wanted to call it – had no mercy.

We drove on in silence. There sure was plenty to think about. Just about the time I started to think about asking Skinner my question about expressing gratitude for life's small mercies – if I ever had the chance, which seemed unlikely – he asked me if I was hungry. I nodded. Then I pictured the waitress double-checking my order, just making sure she got it down right: "So, that was one large, shiny bowl of semen?"

■ ■ ■

We parked in front of the El Serape and woke the girls. Maggie Horton's folks had come to town to straighten out their youngest daughter's affairs. If things worked out, Maggie's sister and her husband were gonna take over the business. While their folks worked out the financial wranglings, the couple kept the doors open.

Other than the two Feds drinking beer at the bar, we were the only customers in the place. We took a table under the big red, blue, and white serape – the only wall decoration that remained, unless you counted the bullet holes made by yours truly. I ordered the El Serape half-pound bison burger with cheese, a slice of peach pie, and a glass of milk. I silently yummed my way through the meal. The pie was so good it almost brought a tear to my eye. After lunch the girls had a burping contest and when Skinner scolded them I said, "Be easy, pardner" and he thought about it, then nodded.

While we waited at the register for change I overheard the agents laughing about how some old cow-poke named Lucky Frank was the new marshal in town. Somehow hearing that made me feel that everything was gonna be getting right back to Pie-Town-normal in no time at all.

I held the door open while the girls hopped into the backseat. I looked back at the El Serape. I thought about my first day on the job. It had been a real good day. I thought about the beautiful red-head – how she'd flushed when I cussed and how she'd scolded me for drinking up the profits. I thought about Alice – how she'd come in just to shoot the shit and I'd have to give her the time-out signal so's she'd shut her yap long enough to take a breath. I thought about Romeo, my hero. I thought about the night I stole Lucky Frank's rifle and shot the place up cuz I wanted Daddy so bad. I wondered: *Was Daddy upstairs pretending to be a cripple while I was downstairs taking pot shots?* I got a knot in the pit of my belly. Things sure had gotten balled up. Then I saw the diner signboard leaning flat against the front of the building. I walked over to give it a look see. HOME OF THE FAMOUS PIE SLICER – that's what it read. And I thought to myself, *Well, I'll be a monkey's uncle*. Maybe I'd mucked things up real good, but here was the proof: I'd left my mark; I'd counted for something. And even if it was only for a short time, well, Pie Town had been a place I could call home. I'd never forget it. Not ever.

Skinner got around into the driver's seat. I stood awkwardly at the curb, then I leaned in and asked him to pop the trunk: I'd just get my box and they could be on their way and I'd be on mine. He started the engine, then reached over and pushed open the passenger door. Tears started to stream down my face: *He was gonna take me with him.*

As we passed Alice's Motel I sniffled and thought about the wide-assed, good-natured proprietor. I pictured her and Mr. Beefy FBI agent . . . maybe he'd stay around and help her run the motel. That sure would be nice for good ole Alice. I wondered why she hadn't come to see me at the hospital, but maybe I knew. A gal like me can only stay on someone's list for so long, and my time on Alice's list was long gone. Besides, in a way, it was a mercy that she didn't come – the weight of her grief and the shameful memories I had of her twins would've preyed something awful on my mind.

I saw Lucky Frank on down the road. He was getting out of a freshly painted ole Studebaker that was parked in the gravel alongside I-60 – parked at about the exact spot where he got taken advantage of but good by one horn-dog of a gal in the middle of the night a while back. The sun reflected off the bright shiny new badge pinned to his vest. As we got closer I pulled my hat down so's he wouldn't see me, but not fast enough. He looked me right in the eyes and gave me the Lucky Frank grin. *That pock-faced old cowboy sure was one lucky son of a gun.*

As we passed the Pie Town Pop. 86 sign, I wondered how long it'd be before they'd adjust that number . . . downward . . . for the dead.

Full tummies and the steady hum and rhythm of the engine lulled the girls into a deep sleep. Did they know their mama was dead? Skinner didn't say and I didn't ask. But if the girls asked me I'd say that she died – but just her body. I'd say her soul was still alive. I'd tell them that one day they'd be walking down a street and they'd stop under a tree and they'd look up and a pretty little bird would be looking right down on them and it would whistle a beautiful tune, and at that moment they'd know for sure that their mama was still alive – they'd know she never really died – and they'd be happy. Did I believe that as a matter of fact? I didn't know. When it came to matters of the spirit, I knew exactly bupkis. Except, well, maybe there was one thing – one thing I learned from the man in the long black coat: when folks turn a flesh-and-blood man into a God, when they assign to this flesh-and-blood man the authority of God – then the odds are pretty good that somewhere down the line some other fella is gonna come along and claim the same of his own flesh and blood. And when that happens, well, *At's a no good*.

As for me and Skinner, I didn't know what was in store for us. His loss was immeasurable. And he'd seen me as low as a gal can go. He'd probably drop me off at the next bus depot and give me a few bucks and tell me to get lost. And I'd get lost. No problem. But if he decided to keep me, well, we'd always have this ugly and unforgiving reality standing between us.

As darkness fell I let myself sink into a bottomless vortex of *what-ifs* and *if-onlys*. And then it hit me like a psychedelic gyration: every single decision I'd made in my life, no matter how small or large, had led me right to this moment. And if I changed even one single decision – no matter big or small – I wouldn't be riding in this car with Skinner. And I realized how easy it would've been to change any one of those millions of decisions

. . . like if I'd decided to wait till another time to go to Anita's, maybe I would've never met greasy ole Daddy. But I didn't wait. I didn't change a thing. I did exactly what I did. And then I let myself drift all the way back to the womb. I thought about all the billions of decisions that had to be made by generations of folks so's that one single egg could be fertilized by one determined little sperm that would eventually give me my life. And just like that, *kowabunga*, it hit me: it was the same for every other person on the face of the Earth – everyone being exactly who they were, and being exactly where they were, and doing exactly what they were doing exactly cuz of every decision that had ever been made in the entire universe. *Holy cow.*

And as for me, well, all those little decisions had brought me right to this very moment: I was riding shotgun in a car with a brokenhearted bear of a man whose suffering was beyond words. In the backseat were two little angels, sleeping soundly. And anyone driving by and caring to sneak a peep through the window would say, "Well now, there's a swell family. Nice. Normal. Look at that: the husband and wife don't even have to talk to each other because they know each other so well." And the other person in the car would say, "Yep. They've probably been together so long there's nothing much left to say." And the folk in that passing car would share a slight chuckle and a grasping but sympathetic glance that would reassure them for the briefest moment that all was right with the world: they were just like us and we were just like them. *Boy, I sure never figured I'd end up finding normal this way.*

My tears came like a flood. I was feeling . . . too much. The reports in the newspapers hadn't captured the true horror of what'd happened that day at the ranch – or the days preceding the raid. It had been a massacre – a slaughter of girls and boys whose innocence had been taken from them by a madman. And each and every face of the "amplitude" flashed before my eyes. And then there was Rabbit, Officer Sanchez, even Punchclock. And then there was Mary. *Oh God, poor sweet Mary Ochs.* She hadn't survived me, or the Fourth Wave. And though I had survived – once again – survival comes with a heavy price, measured in unending guilt and shame. *Is the price ever too high to pay?* Apparently not: I was still alive. I took a deep breath. Maybe that which would otherwise kill a gal ends up making her just that much more fearless in the end. Or maybe not.

I looked at my face in the side-view mirror – the fading checkered marks, my sorrowful eyes – and I thought, *Well, I guess I could always look a little worse for the wear.*

Skinner cleared his throat. I bucked up and wiped the dangling snot on my sleeve.

"You know, there's a faith that believes that taking a single life is like destroying an entire universe."

I closed my eyes.

"It also believes that saving a single life is like saving an entire universe. Do you understand?"

I understood, but lost the ability to speak.

He waited a few moments then said, "I've been trying to remember a quote. I can't remember who said it."

Was he gonna quote his pa, the way he used to?

"No, not him," he said, reading my mind. "It goes—"

He choked up.

"It goes like this: *What is evil but good tortured by its own hunger and thirst?*"

I choked up. I wanted to tell Skinner that I knew who'd said those merciful words. I wanted to tell him that it was Gibran. I wanted Skinner to know that I knew the work of the great Lebanese poet. He'd be surprised, of course. He'd be surprised about a lot of stuff, cuz there was lots of stuff that Skinner didn't know about me – stuff he'd never know. Cuz when a gal is consumed with crushing hurt and humiliation there is only enough room in her head for one conversation, and that predictable and self-pitying conversation takes place between herself and herself.

I leaned my head against the window and wept harder. I didn't know if Skinner had recited the words to forgive me, or to forgive his father, or just to help ease his own pain. But it didn't matter either way. He said them, and he said them to me. And after all, who the hell was I to complain? Just Honey McGuinness, a gal who'd take things any way she could get them.

THE END

www.ingramcontent.com/pod-product-compliance
Lightning Source LLC
Chambersburg PA
CBHW061211170626
46809CB00003B/1320